"What are you doing?"

"I'm touching you." Michael let his hand ease slowly up her neck and the back of her head, sifting her blue-black hair between his open fingers. "How long has it been since a man touched you?"

"That's none of your business."

He kept his hand in her silky hair. "No, it's not. My only business is to make you want my touch."

"Then you'll be waiting till Gabriel blows his horn. I don't care for philandering men."

Clemmie had never met a man his equal in boldness. It wasn't so much that he outraged her, she thought. What was bothering her most was that she liked it. He was stoking some primitive fires in her, and she didn't know what would happen if she let them get out of control....

D0034032

Dear Reader,

Welcome to Silhouette—experience the magic of the wonderful world where two people fall in love. Meet heroines who will make you cheer for their happiness, and heroes (be they the boy next door or a handsome, mysterious stranger) who will win your heart. Silhouette Romance reflects the magic of love—sweeping you away with books that will make you laugh and cry, heartwarming, poignant stories that will move you time and time again.

In the coming months we're publishing romances by many of your all-time favorites, such as Diana Palmer, Brittany Young, Sondra Stanford and Annette Broadrick. Your response to these authors and our other Silhouette Romance authors has served as a touchstone for us, and we're pleased to bring you more books with Silhouette's distinctive medley of charm, wit and—above all—*romance*.

I hope you enjoy this book and the many stories to come. Experience the magic!

Sincerely,

Tara Hughes
Senior Editor
Silhouette Books

PEGGY WEBB

A Gift for Tenderness

Published by Silhouette Books New York

America's Publisher of Contemporary Romance

For my dear friends and pottery teachers,
Euple and Titus Riley

SILHOUETTE BOOKS
300 E. 42nd St., New York, N.Y. 10017

Copyright © 1989 by Peggy Webb

All rights reserved. Except for use in any review,
the reproduction or utilization of this work in
whole or in part in any form by any electronic,
mechanical or other means, now known or
hereafter invented, including xerography,
photocopying and recording, or in any information
storage or retrieval system, is forbidden without
the permission of Silhouette Books, 300 E. 42nd St.,
New York, N.Y. 10017

ISBN: 0-373-08681-4

First Silhouette Books printing October 1989

All the characters in this book are fictitious. Any
resemblance to actual persons, living or dead, is
purely coincidental.

®: Trademark used under license and
registered in the United States Patent and
Trademark Office and in other countries.

Printed in the U.S.A.

Books by Peggy Webb

Silhouette Romance

When Joanna Smiles #645
A Gift for Tenderness #681

PEGGY WEBB

grew up in a large northeastern Mississippi family in which the Southern tradition of storytelling was elevated to an art. "In our family there was always a romance or a divorce or a scandal going on," she says, "and always someone willing to tell it. By the time I was thirteen, I knew I would be a writer."

Over the years Peggy has raised her two children—and twenty-five dogs. "Any old stray is welcome," she acknowledges. "My house is known as Dog Heaven." Recently her penchant for trying new things led her to take karate lessons. Although she was the oldest person in her class and one of only two women, she now has a blue belt in Tansai Karate. Her karate hobby came to a halt, though, when wrens built a nest in her punching bag. "I decided to take up bird-watching," says Peggy.

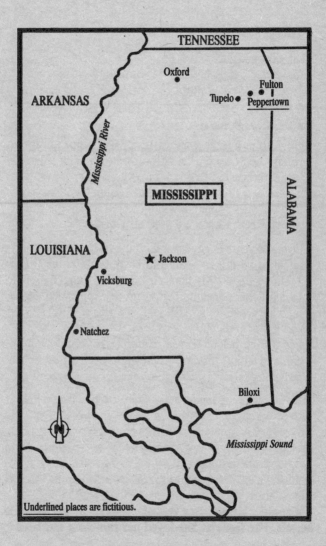

TENNESSEE

ARKANSAS

Oxford

Fulton
Tupelo Peppertown

Mississippi River

MISSISSIPPI

ALABAMA

LOUISIANA

★ Jackson

Vicksburg

Natchez

Biloxi

Mississippi Sound

Underlined places are fictitious.

Chapter One

Clemmie lit the candles—all thirty of them—and sang "Happy Birthday."

Her voice sounded lonesome in the big old house. As a matter of fact, she *was* lonesome. The twins were off at college, Harvey and his tuba were on their way to symphony rehearsal in Fulton, and Miss Josephine Tobias, who was upstairs, was no company at all. She couldn't hear anything less than a sustained bellow.

Sometimes Clemmie wondered what her life would have been like if her parents hadn't died, if she hadn't moved back to Peppertown to take care of her twin brothers. Today was one of those days. Nothing exciting ever happened in Peppertown. Here she was, thirty years old, and she couldn't scare up an adventure or a romance if forty-five pygmies had her trussed up and staked out to burn.

Clemmie sighed. Not that she was unhappy, she told herself. Far from it. She loved her rambling old house;

she loved her small town; she even loved the parade of eccentric and sometimes crotchety boarders who came and went in her life. But just once she wished something exciting would happen to her.

She watched all the candles blaze on her cake and thought about a birthday wish. Not that she believed in birthday wishes. Heaven forbid, she was too sensible for that. But they were traditional, and she was trying her best to have a traditional birthday. After dealing with leaky faucets, stopped-up sinks and a budget that never stretched quite far enough to cover the essentials and still have enough left over to get that green silk dress she was craving, she had made up her mind to be as frivolous and decadent as she could be on her birthday. And what could be more decadent than having birthday cake for breakfast?

She closed her eyes.

"I wish—" She stopped in mid-wish. All the things she needed poured through her mind—enough money to repair the roof and still pay the college bills for her twin brothers, a sewing machine that didn't do the satin stitch when it was supposed to overcast, the patience of Job to deal with Miss Josephine... *Frivolity and decadence,* she reminded herself.

She tried again. "I wish I had a man. Somebody besides Harvey and the postman, please. And send him fast, before I'm too old to pucker up."

Laughing at her own foolishness, she leaned over and blew out her candles, all thirty of them, in one single breath.

"Not bad for an old girl." Clemmie applauded herself and cut a huge piece of cake, one with two pink sugar roses on it. She figured if she was going to celebrate, she might as well do it in style. She'd worry about extra pounds tomorrow.

Taking her piece of cake, she sat down at the kitchen table and looked out the window. That old mockingbird in the backyard was helping her celebrate. He was hopping among the autumn leaves on the crab apple tree, singing his heart out. Underneath the tree the tomcat, who belonged next door, was switching his Persian tail, waiting for the bird to hit a sour note and a shaky branch at the same time and fall into his clutches.

Clemmie laughed aloud. Peppertown wasn't New York City, but it was home, and she loved it. Her life was filled with small day-to-day dramas—the cat chasing a bird, Miss Josephine imagining a burglar, one of her brothers winning an intramural track event and the other getting his heart broken in a campus romance. She licked the icing off her top lip, content. Who needed excitement?

She was well into her second sugar rose when the doorbell rang.

"Isn't that just like Harvey to forget his key?" she said to herself.

She put her half-finished cake on the kitchen table and walked into the polished hallway. The doorbell rang again.

"Just a minute, Harvey. I'm coming."

When she opened the door, she almost swooned. Not only was the man standing on her doorstep *not* Harvey, he was the most gorgeous hunk of male flesh she'd ever seen. Now she knew the meaning of burnished gold. He was tall and luscious and burnished gold all over, his skin, his hair, even his eyes. They were a brilliant and startling amber.

"Sorry to disappoint you."

His voice was every bit as glorious as he was.

"Good grief. There's a birthday fairy, after all."

"I beg your pardon?"

Clemmie still couldn't believe what was in front of her. Peppertown hadn't seen a man like him since Spike Rogers had come back from World War I covered with glory and honor and more women than you could shake a stick at. Or so the legend went.

"You're not Harvey." She knew her mouth was open but she couldn't help it. After all, it wasn't every day that a woman got her birthday wish dropped onto her doorstep.

"No. But I'm good at pretending. If I can bring that charming smile back to your face, I'll be Harvey. What's he like?"

"Limp spaghetti."

Clemmie had always known her habit of saying exactly what she thought would someday get her into trouble. Today was the day. The gorgeous stranger was laughing so hard his sides were shaking. He was bound to think she was addlepated.

Clemmie had a sudden panicked vision of the stranger not being pleased with a crazy landlord. He might decide to leave. And she couldn't afford the luxury of losing a boarder. She had bills to pay. It would behoove her to forget about being decadent and frivolous and begin thinking like a sane, sensible boarding house owner.

"I know you must think I'm crazy," she said. The sparkle that lingered in the stranger's eyes flustered her even more. She reached up and ran a hand through her hair. "Harvey is a boarder of mine, and when the bell rang, I assumed he had forgotten his key. You...startled me."

Michael Forrest took a full minute to appraise the woman standing in the doorway. She reminded him of a

1920's movie vamp with that cap of sleek black hair, those exotic upward-slanting green eyes and that wonderful bow-shaped mouth, ripe cherry red, sensuous, almost pouting. And yet, with that pink smear on her face, she looked innocent and appealing. A fatal combination. Lord deliver him from innocent-looking women. Most of them had the hearts of barracudas.

Old habits of caution made the back of his neck prickle. Already the woman in the doorway had made him laugh at practically nothing. That was clearly a danger sign. If there had been another place to stay in Peppertown, he would have turned and walked away, but he was stuck with the only accommodations in town.

"I'm sorry I startled you." He tore his gaze away from the woman and glanced around at the peaceful landscape. The entire town, and especially this house, could be the set for *Rebecca Of Sunnybrook Farm*. He'd been told rural Mississippi was like that, but this was his first time to see for himself. He turned his attention back to the woman. "I suppose you didn't hear my car drive up."

"No, I didn't. I'm afraid I was too busy celebrating. Today's my birthday."

Was that a blush he was seeing? He didn't believe it. *Nobody* was that innocent, especially beautiful women. He'd learned that lesson a long, long time ago. In Hollywood there were two ways to survive encounters with women—play the wimp or the macho male. Without changing his expression, he lifted his armor into place and assumed his role of careless rake. It had served him well through the years. It should see him through his stay with this paradox, this guileless vamp.

"Happy birthday, lovely lady." He favored her with a smile that had fooled two movie stars into thinking he wanted to marry them.

"My name is Clementine Brady, owner of Brady's Boarding House. But you can call me Clementine. Most folks do." Clemmie gave him a welcoming smile she hoped would reverse any bad first impressions he'd had and get him to sign her guest book.

Southern hospitality combined with the Southern drawl was lethal, Michael decided. He hardened his heart against both of them.

"Michael Forrest." He bent over her hand in his practised manner. But when his lips touched the remnants of sugar icing clinging there, he almost forgot his act. He hadn't tasted sugar icing since he was five. Quickly he released her hand. "My location manager, George Riker, recommended your boarding house."

Clemmie quickly stuck her hand behind her back. It still tingled where Michael Forrest had kissed it. She felt as if she was suffering from instant senility. She supposed that's what happened to women who were seldom kissed when handsome strangers suddenly started nibbling at their hands. At the moment, she wouldn't have been able to remember George Riker if he'd paraded on her front lawn stark naked. "George Riker?"

"Yes. An earnest, sandy-haired young man."

"I remember him now. He was always so quiet. The perfect boarder. He stayed here about two months ago."

"George is like that. A man of few words. However he did recommend your boarding house—in glowing terms." He smiled that smile again, the one that made her think of being serenaded by choirs of angels while eating chocolate bars with almonds. "I hope you have a room."

"For how long?"

"A week, maybe longer. I'll be laying the groundwork for a movie we're going to film here."

"You're in the movie business?"

"Yes. Forrest Productions. Mine is an independent company."

"How did you ever find Peppertown?"

"By good fortune." His incredible amber eyes raked her from head to toe. She felt hot all over, and was absolutely certain that Michael Forrest had invented sex. "Very good fortune, indeed," he added.

Clemmie forced herself to keep in mind that the man was a boarder, a *paying* customer. But casting herself into the role of innkeeper when Hollywood was standing on her doorstep was very hard. "I do have a room." She stilled the trembling in her hands against the door as she held it wide. "Won't you come in?"

He came inside, and suddenly the hallway seemed dowdy to her. The wallpaper looked even more faded beside his bold good looks. But Clemmie had her pride. She lifted her chin and looked him squarely in the eye. "I hope you don't mind an upstairs room, Mr. Forrest."

"Call me Michael."

"All right. Michael."

The way she said his name, soft and drawn out in almost three syllables, made his heart kick against his ribs. His armor had never stood the test against a Southern woman. He'd heard they were lethal. Looking at the woman beside him, he believed the tales. It was time to pull out all the stops with his act. He'd be the biggest cad she'd ever met. He'd woo her and seduce her and outrage her. He'd even make her think he wanted her in his bed, which was the last place he wanted her—or any other woman, for that matter. He still bore the battle scars from his affair with Hubbard, and that had been three years ago.

He took stock of Clemmie again—the exotic green eyes, the silky black hair, the soft skin that drove a man crazy with want to touch it. Nothing less than the full act would protect him against her. When he'd finished, there would be no doubt in her mind that Michael Forrest's intentions were strictly dishonorable.

"I don't mind any room at all, Clemmie, as long as you're within calling distance."

He felt only a slight tinge of regret at the lovely blush that crept into her cheeks. It was surely just an act, he thought. Much like his own.

"Then follow me, please. I hope you like a room with a view."

Clemmie gave a running commentary as she led him up the stairs. "The house is quiet now with only Miss Tobias here. You'll be next door to her. Harvey lives downstairs. He's a tuba player, but he's very considerate about his practice hours. My twin brothers are in college now, but they'll be home some weekends. Four of my permanent boarders aren't here. They are teachers, and they've all gone to a conference in St. Louis."

Michael was sorry when she stopped talking. That soft Southern voice was soothing, like being caressed by angel wings.

"Here it is. Your room with a view."

Clemmie stood in the open doorway, smiling. Michael saw that she had a lot to smile about. The room was filled with antiques, sunlight and charm. It reminded him of a movie set for *Cat On A Hot Tin Roof*. The colors of October—russet and gold and sun-burnished green—spilled through the wide expanse of windows. In the distance, a white heron rose off the sparkling blue surface of a lake. Michael couldn't have been happier if he'd planned the setting himself.

"It's magnificent."

"I'm glad you like it." Clemmie looked around the room, trying to see it through his eyes. When she came to the big brass bed, she imagined how Michael Forrest would look there, stretched out between the sheets, possibly naked. Her cheeks got hot and she spoke in a rush to cover her embarrassment over her thoughts. "I suppose it's quite different from Hollywood. You are from Hollywood, aren't you? Most movie producers are. Well, I suppose they are. I don't know any. Except you, of course."

Her flustered, breathless manner amused him. "Yes, I'm from Hollywood, but I prefer this view."

He wasn't looking at the view at all. He was assessing her with the delicious, devil-may-care expression on his face that she'd noticed downstairs. She felt flustered and somewhat foolish, being thirty and not knowing what to do when a man looked at you that way.

She cleared her throat. "If you get up early in the morning—"

"I do. Do you?"

"Yes."

"I like to jog. Perhaps you'll join me."

"I don't think—"

"I like to have a companion. Especially one as lovely as you. Besides, I need a guide to show me around Peppertown."

She put a hand on her chest to still her fast-pumping heart. "I was going to tell you about breakfast."

"Tell me about breakfast." He came toward her in that hero's way he had of walking, sort of nonchalant and suggestive at the same time, came so close she could feel his body heat. "I have a hearty appetite. For all things."

Clemmie's breath caught in her throat so that she could barely speak above a whisper. "Then you'll enjoy the plantation breakfast we serve at Brady's Boarding House.''

"I plan to enjoy everything at Brady's Boarding House."

She longed for every deliciously wicked thing his voice implied. And she didn't have the foggiest idea what to do about it. Seven years of living in a town of two hundred as a pillar of the community and a model of responsibility and decorum had not prepared her for romance and adventure with a Hollywood hero. But she was for darned sure going to learn. A man like Michael Forrest only came through every seventy years or so, and if she waited for the next one she'd be too old. Or dead.

"It's my job to see that you do," she said with determined spunk.

"A perfect arrangement."

"Breakfast is served in the downstairs dining room between seven and eight. Family style. You are responsible for all your other meals. Woody's Cafe is down the road. About two blocks if we had blocks to count. Hot coffee and tea are available any time."

"And you?" He stepped so close she could see the faint shadow of his beard, as if he'd traveled all night and not had time to shave. It was very sexy. "In case I need to ask directions..." he said smoothly, his smile as wicked as sin. "...or anything." His voice was pure seduction.

Talking was an effort for her and sounding sensible was a miracle. "I live downstairs. My office hours are posted on the door, but I'm usually around in case of an emergency. Except on Wednesdays."

"What do I do if I need you on Wednesday?"

The way he said "need" made her mouth water. "I work as church secretary on Wednesday. The church is just two miles up the road."

Michael chuckled. "I love the way everything is up the road or down the road here. No freeway traffic to battle. It must make life very peaceful."

"Peaceful but unexciting."

"Do you like excitement, Clemmie?"

She laughed. "The most exciting thing I've done lately is go to the funeral home in Fulton with Miss Tobias to pick out her casket. She even insisted on climbing in one of them and trying it out for comfort. Fortunately for both of us, the funeral director, Mr. Landerford, was very understanding."

He took her hand and lifted it to his lips. "I'll try to do better than that, Clemmie." His tongue flicked over the sticky spot where the sugar roses had been. "You taste like strawberries."

Nobody had ever licked her hand. She glanced at his face with alarm. He had a steamy seductive expression she'd only seen in the movies. There was no telling what this gorgeous Hollywood man would do next. She probably could have handled a handsome stranger from Fulton, but one from Hollywood was a different story. She pulled her hand away. "There's more where that came from."

"There is?"

"The cake, I mean. I have plenty of birthday cake downstairs if you'd like some."

"I'd enjoy it very much." He calculated the effect his act was having on her. He'd never seen a woman react so strongly. If she was playing the role of innocent, she was playing it to the hilt. And it was getting to him. He decided to give them both a little relief. "I'll join you after I retrieve my gear from that stubborn piece of junk they call a rental car."

Clemmie got through the door and down the stairs and all the way into the kitchen before she gave vent to her feelings. Leaning her head against the door, she whispered, "Heaven help me." She was giddy and shaking, elated and scared all at the same time. Nothing like Michael Forrest had ever happened to her. She was totally unprepared for a sophisticated man, but the thrill of the unknown beckoned to her.

With slow determination she approached her pantry and pulled open the door. Rows and rows of glass jars lined the shelves—pickled peaches and plum jelly and green tomato relish and pear honey. She'd prepared and canned it all, every jar. That's how she spent her summers.

She thought of her sewing machine upstairs in the third floor attic room. On cold winter days she sewed, partly to pass the time away and partly out of necessity. She made her own dresses and skirts and blouses. She even made shirts for the twins.

Beside the sewing machine was her hobby table. She shut her eyes and pictured it, filled with crooked ceramic bulldogs and tangled macrame wall hangings and lopsided pottery vases. Her hobbies helped pass the long, quiet evenings when there was nothing to do in Peppertown except listen to the frogs croak—and nobody to do it with.

Soberly she closed the pantry doors. Her life could be measured by canning jars and homemade clothes and amateur clay pots. And she was ready for a change. More than ready. Hungry. Yes, she thought. That was a better description.

Opportunity in the form of Michael Forrest had walked straight through her door, and she was determined to do something about it. Not that she had visions of anything permanent, heaven forbid. She had responsibilities—putting the twins through school, making ends meet, keeping the family home intact in the town they all loved so dearly. And anyway, Hollywood was a different world.

But it would be lovely to have a handsome man to take to the church social. They might even get to know one another well enough to spend some cozy evenings in the parlor, playing checkers…and exchanging a kiss or two.

She was still blushing at that thought when Michael Forrest walked through the door. She hoped he didn't read minds.

He stopped and lingered against the door frame, taking in the scene. His gaze lingered on Clemmie while her blush deepened, then moved to the cake. "I haven't seen sugar roses since I was five years old."

"I made them myself. Birthday cakes are one of my specialties."

"And what are your others, Clemmie?"

"Corn chowder and biscuits and French pastry."

He thought briefly of all the West Coast golden girls whose specialties were surfing and flirting and naughty games. Clemmie was as fresh to him as a stiff breeze off the Pacific. Careful, he warned himself.

He left the doorway and stalked her. When he was close enough to see the tiny gold flecks in the middle of her green eyes, he stopped and smiled down at her.

"I'm dying to taste your French pastry."

She felt her toes curl under. The way he said "French pastry" made her think of something risqué. Her tongue clung to the roof of her dry mouth and all logical thought left her head. She had a sudden wish that opportunity could have come in a less intimidating form.

Remembering that she was thirty years old, for goodness' sake, and had had a romantic experience, even if it was only sweaty kisses in the back seat of Johnny Lackey's Thunderbird more years ago than she cared to remember, Clementine Brady pulled herself together.

"I'm afraid you'll have to wait. French pastry day is Tuesday."

"I can hardly wait." He chuckled at the stiff back she presented when she walked to the cabinet. The china plates rattled as she delved among them. She actually seemed nervous. He relented a little. "Let's be friends, Clemmie."

She came back to the table with two china plates. "I'd like that." Her face was bright as she cut two slices of cake. She added an extra sugar rose to his plate.

Michael took a bite of the confection. Watching her as intently as a big cat watches a mouse hole, he flicked his tongue around his lips and provocatively licked off the excess sugar.

She got butterflies in her stomach.

"Do you like it?" she asked.

"Indeed I do. I can never resist sweets...of any kind."

She folded her hands tightly together in her lap and tried to keep her composure. "Then I think you'll enjoy our church socials. Mrs. Langtree makes the best chocolate cream pie in town." Her cheeks turned pink again as his sexy tongue flicked another speck of sugar off his lips. "That is," she continued nervously, "if you want to go."

His fork clanked against the china as he put it aside. Propping his elbows on the table, he leaned so close that she could see a tiny muscle twitching in his fine, square jaw.

"Is that an invitation?"

"No...yes...I don't know."

He smiled. "Do I bother you, Clemmie?"

She cleared her throat as she briefly considered lying. In the end she decided on the truth. "Yes."

"Why?"

"Most of the men I know are..." She paused, searching for the right word.

"Limp spaghetti?"

They laughed together.

"I guess you could say that."

"Most of the women I know are not as honest as you. I like that." He picked up his fork and lifted another sugar rose to his lips. "I like that very much."

Clemmie began to relax. "So you came to Mississippi to film a movie?"

"Yes. A horror movie. You have some great bogs here along the Tombigbee River, and I want to use a small Southern community. Peppertown is perfect."

"You seem awfully young to be a movie producer. I always picture them as old and fat and balding and paunchy."

"I'm one of the new breed, Clemmie. I practically grew up on the movie set. There was never anything else I considered doing."

"Your childhood must have been very exciting."

"It was as exciting as hell."

And about as much fun, he thought. His home had been an armed camp with his spoiled movie star mother and his egotistical writer father on opposite sides of the field, engaged in pitched battle. Fortunately for him, he was usually off at some snobbish, expensive camp or school. There it didn't matter that nobody loved him. The only thing that mattered was not letting the camp director or the headmaster find out what he was really thinking.

With Clemmie's clear green eyes watching him, he felt churlish. Hell, he thought, why spoil her birthday with the truth? Smiling, he began to edit his childhood. "My mother is Melody Raintree—"

"The star of *How Great The Earth*?"

"She's the one. Dad wrote movie scripts, mostly for her. We traveled a lot. Home was often a trailer on location." He could tell by the expression on her face that she thought his life had been glamorous. Glamour and mystery suited him fine. It had always served as a convenient cover for the truth.

Watching Clemmie, he found himself being curious about her background. He knew it was a bad sign. Men intent on avoiding emotional entanglements should never try to understand women. But looking into those compelling eyes, he decided to break his own rule. Just this once.

"What about you, Clemmie? How did a beautiful woman like you end up in a small place like Peppertown?"

"I was born here. I've lived here all my life except for the two months I lived in Atlanta, right after I graduated from college."

In spite of his intentions to keep an emotional distance, he was intrigued. "Atlanta's a swinging city. And about as unlike Peppertown as any city can be. Is it true that most country girls long for the big city lights?"

"Perhaps." Clemmie loved talking with her boarders. It was one of the simple joys of her work. She supposed she was too open about herself and talked entirely too much, but what was the harm? She smiled at Michael. "I suppose that adage about the grass being greener on the other side of the fence is true. It was in my case. I could hardly wait to live in a place where taxicabs outnumbered crickets.''

"And yet you stayed only two months?"

"My parents were killed in an accident."

He felt a sudden urge to take her in his arms and hug away that little-lost-girl look. He actually stiffened his back to keep himself from doing so. "I'm sorry, Clemmie. That must have been damned hard for you."

"Not so hard. I had my brothers and this lovely old home. I came back to take care of David and Daniel."

"Lucky guys."

"Thank you. You're kind."

He'd never known how dangerous sweet women were. With a great effort, he abandoned his attempt at friendship and slid into his role of Michael the Ladykiller.

"No. I'm never kind, Clemmie, only predatory." He reached out and took her hand. "I suppose I'll have to fight half a dozen men off to get into your bed."

Her face flamed so hot she thought the roots of her hair might catch fire. She fought for her composure and her hand. She lost both battles.

"Are you always so brazen, Mr. Forrest?"

"Always, especially when I see something I want."

"And what is it that you want?"

"You."

"Well, for goodness' sake. I've never—"

"No," he interrupted smoothly, "probably not."

"The men I know are gentlemen . . ."

"Limp spaghetti," he corrected, chuckling.

"They have manners and morals. Goodness gracious, for all I know, you might even be married."

He tipped back his head and roared. None of the women he knew had ever given a damn whether he was married. Their only concern was the size of his bank account.

"You're delightful, my darling Clementine."

"You're outrageous." She rose from her chair, lifted her chin and glared down at him. "Just to think. I was considering inviting you into my parlor to play checkers."

"I don't need an invitation, Clemmie. I take what I want."

Chapter Two

She stalked out of the kitchen and up the stairs, his words ringing in her ears: "I take what I want." What he wanted was to be in her bed. She was so flustered she forgot a lifetime of training in good Southern manners. Her guest was left to fend for himself in the kitchen.

She paused midway up the stairs and put a hand over her pounding heart. "Well, for goodness' sake," she said aloud. Then, as she continued, "Good grief." What she had wished for was a hero on a white charger. What she got was a knight in tarnished armor.

Clementine Brady was out of her league and she knew it. Her sole romantic experience had been with Johnny Lackey. They'd grown up in Peppertown together, gone to school together, and shared their first kiss. By the time they were seniors, they'd become engaged. She went off to college and he went off to Columbus Air Force Base. They'd remained true and faithful to each other, writing letters twice a week and longing for his furloughs. During those times they held hands until their knuckles were white and kissed until the car windows were steamy.

The future was bright for them. She was a year away from graduation and a fine job in journalism; he had his pilot's wings. They set a wedding date. Six months later his plane malfunctioned on a training mission over the Gulf of Mexico. He went down in the flaming wreckage.

Somehow she got through her graduation. She worked long and hard in Atlanta, trying to forget. And then, after only two months at her new job, her parents' car had blown a tire on Highway 78 and veered under an eighteen-wheeler.

Clemmie had come back to Peppertown. The community that had nurtured her now comforted her. In the quiet tranquillity of the red clay hills of northeast Mississippi, she had healed.

Nothing had marred her peace. Neither had there been any excitement. Until today. Until Michael Forrest had walked through her door.

She stopped on the second floor landing and took a deep breath. She was flabbergasted and flustered and scared out of her wits. But more than that, she was intrigued. Like a child who reaches out to a hot stove, she was drawn to Michael Forrest.

And she was going to do something about it. As soon as she could get her heart back to normal and her breathing regulated, she was going to march right back downstairs and invite him to that church social. Propriety and Southern manners be hanged.

Clemmie had her hand on the door to the attic stairs when Josephine Tobias picked up the cowbell beside her chair and shook it vigorously. The loud clanging sent Clemmie hurrying to Josephine's bedroom.

"I saw him from the window," the old woman said before Clemmie had time to get into the room.

Clemmie shut the door and crossed the room until she was standing directly in front of Josephine. Leaning down, she shouted close to her ear, "Who did you see?"

"Shoes on a bee?" Josephine reached out a wrinkled hand and felt Clemmie's forehead. "Lord, child, you'd better stay away from that attic. You're getting as addlepated as me."

Clemmie cupped her mouth and shouted louder, "You said you saw a man at the window."

Josephine leaned back, her face as faded and yellow as the dried rose corsage on her dress. "No. I didn't see a van; I saw a man."

"When?"

"Glen? No, he's off in St. Louis at that teacher's conference, I think. Didn't he tell you he was going?"

"Of course."

"On a horse? No. I think they took a plane. St. Louis is a mite far to go on a horse."

Clemmie gave up. She took a step back. "If you need me for anything else, just ring."

She wasn't sure whether Josephine understood the words or merely the attitude of dismissal. In any case, she unfolded a paper on her lap and thrust it at Clemmie.

"That's him. Right there. I was at the window watching the birds when he rang the bell."

Clemmie smiled. Josephine Tobias had no more been watching the birds than she could fly. She'd been spying. It was her favorite pastime. That and reading gossip tabloids like the one she was holding out now—*Secrets Of The Rich And Famous*. The title of the tabloid was printed in huge red letters across the front page.

Josephine shook the paper. "His picture is right there in black and white."

Everything clicked in Clemmie's mind. With Josephine's combined talents for snooping and reading gossip, she'd naturally have made the connection between their latest boarder and the latest scandal sheet. Curious now, Clemmie took the paper.

"Movie Mogul Denies Children," the headline proclaimed. Underneath was a close-up of Michael Forrest on the set of what appeared to be a monster movie.

Clemmie scanned the story, picking up key phrases. "Michael Forrest slapped with not one, but two, paternity suits...denies both children...longtime live-in Hubbard Gladstone claims Michael is the father. Melody Raintree...heartbroken. Famous star longs to be a grandmother...severed all ties with Don Juan son... scandal dogs controversial producer...famous Hollywood beauty Jinx Maxy files palimony suit. What next for this famous son of a famous mother?"

Clemmie folded the tabloid slowly and carefully, trying to control her shaking hands. She had never believed half of what those papers printed. The trick was to separate truth from innuendo.

"Well," Josephine demanded. "Are you going to let him stay?"

Clemmie wavered. She'd never turned anyone away from her boarding house. In Peppertown it had never been necessary to ask for references. Her boarders had always been as law abiding and trustworthy as the town's citizens. Deep down, she didn't want to believe all she'd read about Michael Forrest. Still, he had vowed to bed her.

She felt hot all over. Two women pregnant and one suing for palimony. For a moment she imagined herself as Michael's lover. If she got pregnant, he'd deny the child, just as he had his others.

The whole town would be scandalized. Her brothers would be outcasts in decent society. And the poor helpless baby. She didn't even want to think about that.

"Before we can say Jack Rabbit," Josephine continued, "we'll all be scandalized in our beds, pregnant as a house."

The ludicrous idea of eighty-year-old Miss Josephine Tobias being pregnant as a house brought Clemmie back to her senses.

She tossed the paper aside.

"This is all nonsense."

"No defense. That's what I say. We poor helpless women will have no defense against a man who philanders with everything in skirts." Josephine paused long enough to pat the dead corsage on her shoulder. "What will my poor departed Junior Wade say about that?"

Clemmie stifled a chuckle. Junior Wade had been Miss Josephine's lover for thirty years. Although he'd been dead for another thirty, she still referred to him as if they had daily conversations. "You'll be safe as a church," she shouted. "I promise you that."

"I smell a rat, too. And his name is Michael Forrest."

She patted Josephine's hand. "Don't you worry a minute. I'll take care of everything."

"I'd demand a ring, too, before I'd let him lift my skirts."

Clemmie gave up. Trying to talk with Miss Josephine was as confusing as stepping through Alice's looking glass.

She waved goodbye to Josephine and went back into the hallway. She hardly knew what to do. When she'd asked for excitement, she'd gotten more than she bargained for. Her Southern Baptist upbringing hadn't prepared her to deal with a man like Michael Forrest.

She amended her earlier wish for every wicked thing his seductive voice suggested. What she wanted now was merely to survive his invasion into her quiet, orderly life without appearing too foolish or too naive.

Instead of going to the top floor and her sewing machine as she had planned, she hurried back down the stairs, peering beyond the balcony railing to make sure Michael Forrest didn't spot her. She made it safely to her room without being seen. Then she began to pace the floor and ponder what to do. On the one hand, she'd never had a boarder as scandalous and notorious as Michael. Shoot, she thought. For all she knew, he might even be dangerous. On the other hand, she needed the money. She'd had a letter just yesterday from David. He had to get new track shoes and Daniel needed fifty dollars to buy geology equipment.

She'd confront Michael, she decided. But what would she say? To bolster her courage, she faced the mirror and practised what she would say. "Mr. Forrest, I know all about you." Disgusted, she whirled away from the mirror and paced the room. That wouldn't do. It was too accusatory. She came back and tried again. "Mr. Forrest, we have certain standards here at Brady's Boarding House." No. Too prim and prissy. She made another circuit around the room, took a deep breath and tried again. "Michael..." That was better. Friendlier. Less remote. "I've never had occasion to dismiss a boarder..." That was ridiculous. She couldn't kick Michael Forrest out even if she wanted to. He was too big. And probably too mean. And certainly too intimidating.

All her pacing and practicing made her hot. She went to the window to let in an Indian summer breeze. Michael Forrest was in her backyard, sitting in her gazebo, feet propped on the railing, acting as if he owned the whole thing. She could imagine the scuff marks his shoes were making against the paint. And she'd just put a fresh coat on last summer.

Her first impulse was to lean out the window and tell him to take his feet down; but remembering the article, she changed her mind. There was no telling what he might do.

She'd started to pull back from the window when he saw her. He stood up with that easy, lazy grace she noticed earlier.

"Looking for me, Clemmie?"

"Yes—" Stopping, she wondered what reason she would give. "No," she amended quickly.

Smiling, he lifted one of his cocky eyebrows. "Which is it, my darling Clementine? Yes or no?"

"No."

He left the gazebo and started toward her window. "I'm disappointed, but not deterred." When he was less than a foot from her open window, he stopped. Suddenly he dropped to one knee and gazed up at her. "'Oh, wilt thou leave me so unsatisfied?'"

She was so enchanted by his dramatic rendition of Romeo's complaint beneath the balcony that she responded automatically with Juliet's sensible reply. "'What satisfaction canst thou have tonight?'"

"Enough satisfaction to leave us both panting."

"That's not Romeo."

"You're far more delectable than Juliet." He stood up and leaned against her windowsill. "Where did you learn Shakespeare?"

"The same place you did. From a book."

"Bravo, Miss Brady. I love a woman with spirit."

She knew she shouldn't let his compliment go to her head, but she couldn't help herself. Her common sense took a back seat to her ego. For the moment she forgot Michael Forrest's indiscretions.

"I enjoy a man who can quote Shakespeare."

"And I enjoy a woman who can blush." He reached through the window and touched her cheeks. "You're very appealing with your cheeks flushed like that and your eyes sparkling."

She was foolishly glad that she hadn't put up screens last summer as she'd intended to. She briefly relished the warmth of his hand before she pulled back. "Don't."

"Why not?"

"Because...I'm not like that." She reached up for the window, but he kept his hand on the sill. She couldn't let the window down without squashing his fingers, and she was too polite to do that.

"Like what, Clemmie?"

"Those Hollywood women."

He smiled. "Thank God for that."

Clemmie thought his reaction was strange. In her mind, all Hollywood women were glamorous and gorgeous and sophisticated and willing—all the things she was not. She couldn't imagine a man like Michael Forrest wanting anything different. Before she could tell him so, he was talking again.

"You don't know how tired I am of Hollywood women."

For a moment the devil-may-care expression was gone from his face. He looked like a man who had lost too much and was mourning that loss. With an insight and a compassion given to those who live close to the land, Clemmie saw that success had not been without a price for Michael Forrest. Neither had notoriety.

Her maternal instinct rose, and she almost reached out to put a soothing hand on Michael's brow. She was saved the gallant gesture by his next glib words.

"Fortunately it's only a temporary condition. I'm sure that by the time I leave Peppertown, I'll be fully recovered."

"I don't intend to provide the cure," she said, and she reached for the top of the window again. This time, she began to jerk it down.

Michael jumped back. She slammed the window with a force out of proportion to need, and was rewarded by the alarmed rattling of the windowpanes. The sound gave her a small satisfaction.

She'd intended to turn her back on him and march across the room. It would have been a beautiful exit. But her curiosity overcame her good intentions. She glanced through the window to see Michael's reaction. He was laughing his head off.

"St. Peter's britches," she shouted. It was the strongest phrase she ever used. Usually she reserved it for such situations as Cousin Milly running off with the postman, and Uncle Henry taking up with that sleazy waitress down at Tate McDandie's riverfront bar.

Clemmie was having a bad day and she knew it. But something unusual was happening inside her. She felt revitalized, as if she were a puny philodendron that had been given a shot of root fertilizer and a good dose of water. She'd never felt perkier.

Her step was jaunty as she walked across the room and picked up her purse. She always did her grocery shopping on Friday morning, and today would be no different. Michael Forrest had delayed her, but he wouldn't stop her.

She fished out her car keys as she walked toward the back door, all the while thinking that she'd decide what to do about Michael on her way to the grocery store.

She walked across the backyard to her garage. It was an old-fashioned affair, separate from her large Victorian house. The garage was sturdy enough, and painted as white as Easter to match the house, but it tilted at a crazy angle. It always put her in mind of her Uncle Henry after he'd had one whiskey sour too many.

The garage door had no new-fangled remote controls, no buttons to push. It merely hung there, covering the entrance like a malevolent aluminum eye.

She leaned down, grasped the door handle and pulled. The door stuck, as usual. She jiggled the handle and tried again. Still, the door didn't move.

Putting her purse on the ground, Clemmie leaned down and grasped the stubborn door handle with both hands. She executed a series of twists and jiggles that showed her limber figure to best advantage.

Michael Forrest, leaning indolently against the gazebo, thought she was an entrancing sight. His smile broadened as she stepped back and gave the garage door a swift kick. Then she put her hands on her hips and glared at it.

A good producer always knew the right cues, and that was his. He strolled across the lawn until he was standing directly behind her. She was so intent on trying to scare the garage door into cooperation with her frown that she hadn't heard him.

"Dammit," he said.

She jumped, then turned to stare at him.

"I said it for you." He chuckled at the look of surprise on her face. "I knew you were too much a lady to cuss, so I decided to come across the lawn and do your cussing for you.''

"I don't need you to cuss for me.''

"I know. You can do very well by yourself.'' He laughed again. "What was it you said a few moments ago? St. Peter's britches? It was enough to make my toes curl under.''

"How on earth..." She stopped talking and put her hands on her hot cheeks. "I didn't think anybody heard me.''

"You were standing just inside the window. And you were shouting.''

"I never shout.''

"I beg your pardon, ma'am.'' His bow was as exaggerated as his fake Southern accent. "I'd never contradict a sweet Southern belle. Let's simply say that I have bionic hearing. Like Superman.''

Clemmie couldn't help but laugh at his antics. In this playful mood, he reminded her of her eighteen-year-old brothers. When they were home they were always teasing her about something.

"Do you also have bionic muscles? This garage door is stuck, and I can't seem to get it open.''

"Strength and chivalry are two of my many sterling characteristics.'' He came around her and lifted the stubborn garage door. Clemmie thought he made it look easy.

"Thank you. I could eventually have done it, but it would have taken a while, and I'm already late for my grocery shopping.''

"How can one be late for grocery shopping?''

"I have a strict routine that I follow.''

"Is kissing a part of your routine?" He reached out and lifted a strand of her shiny hair with his index finger. It slid across his skin, silky and alive.

Clemmie stepped back. He saw the sudden widening of her eyes, the slight flaring of her nostrils. The reaction was extreme. For the first time since he'd met her, he decided her innocence wasn't an act. But even so, he couldn't afford to let down his guard.

"Do I frighten you, Clemmie?"

She tilted her chin at a proud angle. "Of course not."

He thought she was a lousy liar, but he decided not to pursue the reasons for her fear. He'd found out long ago that caring too deeply opened the door to heartache.

"Good. Then you won't mind if I go along grocery shopping with you."

"Grocery shopping won't interest you."

"How do you know?"

"I've never known a man who was interested in cabbages."

"It's not the cabbages that interest me; it's the company."

"I always shop alone."

"Not today." He picked up her purse and tucked it into her hand. "Today you're going to have a companion." Something about the look in those wide green eyes softened him. "Don't worry, Clemmie. I won't bite you. At least, not today."

"Well . . ."

"You can point out the sights to me as we drive along. This is my first visit to your part of the country, you know." He could see her weakening. He pressed his advantage. "You would be doing me a big favor."

"I suppose it will be all right."

She glanced up at him. He looked as innocent as it was possible for a handsome celebrity from Hollywood to look. And he *was* new in town, she reasoned. What could happen in a car?

Chapter Three

What happened in the car was as safe as sitting in a Sunday school class, but far more stimulating. That was Clemmie's conclusion as she drove down River Hill Road to the grocery store. She was glad she hadn't let that silly article in *Secrets Of The Rich And Famous* scare her out of taking Michael Forrest on an innocent drive.

They were talking about movie-making.

"I'll bring my production crew here, probably sometime in the next couple of weeks. I'll get permission from one of the local landowners to set up camp in some of these beautiful wooded areas."

"How many people will that be?"

"About seventy-five, not including the actors."

"It's a pity Brady Boarding House doesn't have room for all of you. I could use the money."

One of Michael's cardinal rules was that he never became personally involved in the private matters of the women he pursued. He never inquired about their businesses, their politics, or their families. He was equally silent about his own private affairs. Music, art, sports, current events, theater were the safe topics of conversation he habitually chose.

With Clemmie, though, it was different. He'd already broken the rules with her. Now, as he looked at her lovely profile he realized he was going to break the rules again. He didn't know why. It probably had something to do with this town. Everything seemed unreal here, as if he'd stepped back fifty years into a time of genteel ways and unsophisticated concerns. He'd noticed when he'd stepped into Tupelo's small terminal that people never looked at their watches. No one seemed to be in a hurry to go anywhere. And the speech, he mused. Hearing the soft Southern drawl was like floating on a sea of honey.

He looked at Clemmie and smiled. He'd been doing a lot of that lately. In fact, he'd been doing that since he'd seen her standing in the doorway of Brady's Boarding House.

"Why do you need the money, Clementine?"

"I don't usually talk about things like that with strangers."

"I thought we agreed to be friends."

"That was before."

"Before what?"

"Before I read about you in *Secrets Of The Rich And Famous.*"

She stared straight ahead, concentrating with unnecessary intensity on the road. He was amused. Most women would have been plying him with questions. Not that he would have answered them. He never bothered to defend himself against bad publicity.

"Aren't you going to ask me if it's true?"

"I was going to be a journalist—before Mother and Daddy were killed. There has to be some basis for a story like that."

"You're a brave woman, Clementine."

"Why do you say that?"

"You never know what a man with my wicked reputation will do next." He reached over and touched her cheek. He'd been wanting to touch her since he stepped into the car. With the sunlight pouring through the car windows, her skin was the shade of a luscious ripe peach. He also wanted to taste it, but he refrained. No need to play with fire.

He felt her stiffen, but she didn't jerk away. He figured she was too conscientious to risk that while she was driving. He let his fingers play over the soft skin.

"Your complexion is going to be the envy of every woman who comes from Hollywood. They pay makeup artists a fortune to try to achieve this look."

"Do they succeed?"

Chuckling at her honest vanity, he removed his hands. "No. Nature generally outdoes man's puny efforts." His gaze swung from Clemmie to the tress alongside the road; they were brilliant in October colors that wardrobe mistresses only dream of copying.

Clemmie glanced at him out of the corner of her eye. "Beautiful, isn't it?"

"Yes."

"That's one of the reasons I stay in Peppertown. I probably could make more money working in a large city, but I love the land. And I love my rambling gingerbread house. So do my brothers. After Mother and Daddy were killed, the only way to keep the house was to come back and live in it. I didn't want to let it go, and I couldn't afford two residences. David and Daniel were eleven at the time. They needed stability."

"You sacrificed a career out of love for the land and love for your brothers?"

Her eyes were shining as she glanced briefly in his direction. "I don't consider it a sacrifice. I made a choice, and I've never been sorry."

Michael couldn't remember when he'd seen such goodness in a person. He felt as if he were in the company of an angel. If the feeling had persisted, he would have been uncomfortable with what he was doing. But he had no intention of becoming a reformed rake. Men with scruples got hurt. He saved himself by giving Clemmie a thorough perusal. What he saw was all woman—that smoky hair, so black it was almost blue, those exotic eyes, that kissable vamp's mouth. He was an expert at guessing what kind of body was under a woman's clothes. No angel had ever had curves like Clemmie.

He leaned back against the seat, satisfied.

"This morning you said your life was unexciting."

"Peaceful is a better word. And I'm still not sorry."

He reached across the back of the seat and gently placed his hand on the back of her neck. He felt her muscles tense, but she kept her eyes on the road.

"Relax, Clemmie. I told you that I won't bite you."

"What are you doing?"

"I'm touching you." He let his hand ease slowly up her neck and the back of her head, sifting the blue-black hair between his open fingers. "How long since a man has touched you?"

"It's been . . . That's none of your business."

He kept his hand in her silky hair. "No. It's none of my business. My only business is to make you want my touch."

"Then you'll be waiting till Gabriel blows his horn. I don't care for philandering men."

He chuckled. "You like your heroes to be unblemished?"

"Yes. Johnny was a wonderful man, kind and considerate and . . ." She paused, thinking of the right words to describe Johnny's purity. She doubted if a man like Michael would understand, even if she told him.

"A model of virtue?"

"Yes."

"Who is Johnny?"

"It was a long time ago."

"And yet, you referred to him. Who is he?"

"He was my fiancé."

"Was?"

"He's dead. His fighter plane crashed in the Gulf more than seven years ago."

"I'm sorry, Clemmie." Michael discovered somewhat to his surprise that he really was sorry, not for Johnny because he hadn't known the man, but for Clemmie. He was sorry that she had suffered. And she had. He could tell by the look of vulnerability on her face when she talked of her dead fiancé. He fought his urge to protect her. Such nobility would serve no purpose except to build false hopes in an innocent woman and set the stage for another disappointment for him. Damned nobility, he thought. He'd long since learned that playing the cad was the only way to survive.

"No one can compete with dead heroes, and I don't intend to try." He steeled himself against the shocked outrage in her face. He wanted to say I'm doing this for your own good as well as mine, Clemmie, but he knew she wouldn't understand. Women never did. Instead he moved his hand down the back of her neck and began a tender massage. "Dead heroes can't keep you warm at night. And satisfied. I can." His fingers circled the bunched-up muscles on her neck. "And I will."

Clemmie regretted letting him get into her car. It was not so much that he scared and outraged her, she thought. Although, Lord knows, she'd never met a man his equal in boldness. What was bothering her the most was that she liked it. A part of her responded to his frankly sexual talk. He was stoking some primitive fires in her, and she didn't know what would happen if she let them get out of control.

As his fingers pressed into her flesh, she let her imagination roam. She was lying on a beach somewhere. Hawaii, she decided. She'd always wanted to go there. Michael was stretched out beside her, the sun gilding his golden skin. His hands were on her, stroking her face. They moved downward, toward her breasts. His hands were hot and bold as they moved over her.

She felt her breathing start to become raspy. But she was no longer on the beach in Hawaii; she was in her car in Peppertown.

While she always chose sensible cotton bikinis, Clemmie indulged herself with bras. The one she was wearing today was a mere wisp of sheer nylon. It did nothing to disguise her state of excitement. And Michael Forrest saw exactly what was happening. She could tell by the way his eyes lit up.

She stared straight ahead, trying to get herself back under control.

"It's unusually hot for October," she said.

"Indeed?" He quirked an eyebrow upward.

"Yes. We call it Indian Summer."

"I call it lust."

"What?"

His fingers pressed against her neck. "Lust, Clemmie. It makes people hot."

The headline in *Secrets Of The Rich And Famous* blazed through her mind.

"Remove your hand."

"You don't like being touched?"

"No."

"Your body says yes."

"You shouldn't believe everything you see."

Chuckling, he took his hand away. "I agree."

"You do?" She was vaguely disappointed.

"Yes. I'm a master at inventing reality, but I never make the mistake of believing my own creations. In the movies, Clemmie, seeing is not believing—but seeing is certainly entertaining." His bold glance raked over her.

She concentrated on the road.

"Good grief!" She swerved the car wildly to the left. Michael was pitched against her shoulder. His left arm grabbed her and his right hand pitched against her shoulder. His left arm grabbed her and his right hand grabbed the wheel. They fought for control of the car. Clemmie hit the brakes.

"Don't," Michael said, but it was too late. The car was already swerving off the road.

They jarred against each other as the ancient Buick settled into a shallow ditch. Michael cupped Clemmie's face.

"Are you all right?"

She took a deep shaky breath. "Yes. Are you?"

He figured he'd have a bruise where his knee banged the dashboard, but that didn't count. He smiled at her. "Never better."

He was draped all over her, so close she could see tiny amber sunbursts in the center of his golden eyes. He smelled masculine and intensely sexy, a subtle blend of sea breezes and spice. She took a deep breath and let his scent wash over her. "I'm glad," she whispered. "I wouldn't want to hurt you, even if you are the most aggressive man I've ever met."

"You're sweet, Clemmie." His fingers gently caressed her peach-down cheeks. "Don't be too sweet to me."

She knew there were things she should be doing—getting the car out of the ditch and getting herself out of his clutches, but she was reluctant to move. Sitting there in the stranded vehicle with the sunshine pouring through the window and Michael's hands on her face seemed to be the right thing to do. At least for the moment—until she could get her thinking straight.

"Why, Michael?"

"Because I'm no gentleman. I don't respond to sweetness."

Clemmie thought she saw a certain sadness in his face, and she wondered if anybody in Michael's life had ever been sweet to him, and gentle and kind and understanding. She wanted to cuddle him and take him home and nurture him, just as she would a stray puppy.

Still cupping her face, he bent over and gently brushed her cheeks with his lips. "If we stay in this car any longer, I'll be forced to demonstrate just how much an ungentleman I am." He released her and moved back across the seat. "Unfortunately my style would be cramped by these close quarters, and I've promised not to seduce you today. I suggest we get out and figure a way out of our dilemma."

Clemmie's visions of a stray puppy vanished. Instead she looked across the car seat into the face of a lion, and a hungry one, at that. She felt a trickle of sweat between her breasts. She reached up and pushed her hair away from her hot face.

"That's a relief."

"That I'll help you? I'm not that much an ungentleman."

"No. That you won't seduce me."

He chuckled. "Clementine Brady, how can I seduce you when you keep making me like you?"

"I didn't know seduction and liking were mutually exclusive."

"To me they are."

They both got out of the car. Michael propped his arms on the top and looked across at her. "How did we get into this ditch?"

"A cat."

"You swerved for a cat?"

"Of course."

"I didn't see it."

"No. You were too busy looking at me."

"A blunt woman. I like that."

"Are we going to stand here all day or are we going to get the car out of the ditch?"

"Also a practical woman. I like that, too."

He strolled around the car, assessing the situation.

Clemmie watched him. For seven years she'd had no one to depend on except herself. It was nice to have a man around for a change, especially a man like Michael, who looked as if he could run straight into an army of invading Martians and take charge.

The ditch was shallow, and Michael was strong. They got the car back on the road in a very short while.

Clemmie was both relieved and disappointed that Michael behaved for the rest of the drive. He even helped her with the grocery shopping. Buying cabbages had never been as much fun. As it turned out, Michael Forrest knew quite a bit about food and nutrition. They laughed and joked together with the ease of long-time friends as he gave her advice and shared some of his recipes.

But he swore her to secrecy.

"My reputation would be in ruins if word got out that I'm dispensing recipes instead of kisses."

"My lips are sealed."

He looked at her lips and thought how delicious they would taste. Standing in the frozen food section of the grocery store, he longed to seal her lips in another way—with his. With any other woman, he would have, and the on-lookers be damned. But he instinctively knew that Clemmie would be scandalized. The strange thing to him was that he cared. This innocent woman with the peachdown skin and the trusting eyes had touched some calloused place in his soul, and he was beginning to soften.

Careful, Michael, he told himself. *The next thing you know you'll be developing scruples.* His grip tightened on the grocery cart. The best thing he could do would be to get out of this damned grocery store and out of her sight before he made a complete fool of himself.

"Let's check out the yogurt, Clemmie. I know a hell of a recipe for yogurt cooler."

He took hold of the grocery cart and pushed it down the aisle, the picture of innocence and good manners.

When they returned to the Brady Boarding House, he helped her unload the groceries.

"As much as I'd love to spend the rest of the day promoting my cause, I have to leave you, Clementine. Unfortunately movies don't make themselves." He bent down and gave her a tender kiss on the cheek. " 'Parting is such sweet sorrow.' "

"That's my line, Romeo." She loved the way his eyes lit up.

" 'Sleep dwell upon thine eyes,' " he quoted softly, " 'peace in thy breast. Would I were sleep and peace, so sweet to rest.' "

Without another word, he was gone.

She went to the front door and watched until his rental car was out of sight.

"Michael Forrest, I do believe you're a fraud." Unconsciously she caressed the door handle that he'd so recently touched. "You're a lovable tabby cat masquerading as a ferocious lion."

The idea pleased her enormously. She began thinking once more about the church social. She would probably invite him after all.

Clemmie was too busy to think about her latest boarder for the rest of the day. She ate her lunch; she planned breakfast menus for next week; she wrote to her brothers; she took Miss Josephine Tobias to the dentist. That proved to be an all-afternoon affair.

It was almost dark when they got back. She noticed that Michael's car was still gone.

As she helped Miss Josephine up the stairs, she decided the house seemed quieter without Michael, duller, even shabbier. The house seemed old and tired. Like me, she thought. Maybe she and the house both needed a good dose of whatever magic Michael Forrest was dispensing. What had he said in the car? That he was a master of inventing reality. As she matched her steps to Miss Josephine's tired shuffle, she decided that it would be lovely if she could forget her responsibilities for a few days and be caught up in a Michael Forrest fantasy.

After having spent the afternoon scouting locations, Michael was enjoying his first fried catfish meal at Woody's Cafe in what he supposed was the center of Peppertown. The small restaurant was neat and clean, with polished brass fixtures, quiet Wedgwood blue walls and starched Priscilla curtains. About fifteen people sat at the small Formica-topped tables around Michael, and they all seemed to know each other.

Conversation whizzed from table to table, buzzing around him like excited insects. During the course of his meal, Michael overheard remedies for bad colds—not merely colds, he mused, but *bad* colds. Mustard plasters and castor oil were the answers. He learned how to trap gophers: put chewing gum in the hole and cover it with a board. He found out that Mary June had left Claude for a traveling preacher and that everybody in the community was ready to tar and feather her if she showed her face around here again. He heard that the new song leader at the Baptist church couldn't hit high C if his life depended on it.

Michael sat back and listened to the day-to-day tribulations of the soft-spoken Mississippi townspeople. It all sounded so wonderfully ordinary and so damned innocent. Like Clemmie. His mind swung back to the woman he'd vowed to keep at arm's length with less than honorable tactics. How that innocence of hers hammered at his defenses! He wondered if she would have been different if she'd lived in Hollywood where people were cutthroat and problems were high-powered—and where confidences often brought lawsuits.

"Would you like some more of that sweetened tea?"

He glanced up, startled out of his reverie by the quiet drawl of the pretty little waitress. Her wide smile showed two chipped teeth.

"I noticed a while back that you'd finished drinkin' what you had." Without waiting for a response, she refilled his glass. "You're a stranger in town, aren't you?"

Why should you care? he thought. But he could see that she did. Her face was shining with earnestness.

"Yes," he said.

His short answer didn't discourage her. Before he knew what was happening, she'd found out who he was and why he was there and was introducing him to everybody in the restaurant. They folded him to their collective bosom like a long-lost friend. Somebody clapped him on the back, somebody else paid for his dinner, and a fat woman in black started a party. It began with joke-telling and clapping, and ended with a singathon.

Not a soul in the cafe seemed to care a whit about his bank account. And when he mentioned that the loud party might draw some criticism from neighbors, he was told that folks in Peppertown sang when they were happy—and everybody understood.

He was still singing when he got into his car to go back to Brady's Boarding House. He didn't know what time it was and he didn't care. He hadn't felt this relaxed and this happy since he was ten years old.

It was midnight when Michael returned to the house.

Clemmie heard his car drive up. She closed the book she had been reading and walked to the bedroom window. She hadn't really been waiting up for him, she told herself. But he *was* her boarder, and she felt a certain duty to see that he was all right.

The moon, bright as only an October moon can be, shone down on him as he got out of the car. Clemmie sucked in her breath. She'd never seen a man who looked so like a Greek god. He was golden and beautiful.

He was also singing.

He strolled toward the gazebo, his face lifted toward the moon, singing in a lusty baritone.

"Oh my darlin', oh my darrrlin', oh my darrrlin', Clem-en-tine."

She threw open the window and leaned out.

"Be quiet, you'll wake the other boarders."

Michael turned around. When he saw her, his face lit in a broad grin. " 'But, soft! What light through yonder window breaks? It is the east, and Juliet is the sun.' "

"It's midnight, and I'm the innkeeper."

" 'Arise fair sun—' "

"You're crazy."

"No, I'm merely giving vent to the spontaneous joy your little town brings out in me. Somebody started a singathon at Woody's and I can't seem to stop." He waved his arm toward her. "Come out and join me."

"Shh! Do you want everybody to hear?"

"I was told that everybody in Peppertown loves a happy person. Won't you come out, darling Clementine?"

Clemmie heard an upstairs window open.

"What's going on down there?" Miss Josephine's quavery voice drifted down to them.

Clemmie was thankful Miss Josephine's night vision was poor.

"It's just an old tomcat," she called.

"Well, whatever it is, give it what it wants so it'll go home." The upstairs window banged shut.

Michael Forrest, leaning against the gazebo, laughed. "Are you going to give me what I want, Clemmie?"

"I'm going to come out there and drag you off to bed so you won't wake the neighbors."

"I can hardly wait."

Chapter Four

Clemmie hung out the window, her face flaming hot. Goodness gracious. What had she said? That she was going to drag Michael Forrest to bed? He probably thought she was some kind of shady lady.

Closing her eyes, she put her hands to her flushed cheeks and tried to decide what to do. One thing was certain: she had to put a stop to that singing or she'd have Miss Josephine to deal with again.

Michael's humming drifted on the night breeze. She snapped her eyes open and risked a peek in his direction. He was leaning against the gazebo, grinning like that old tomcat next door when he'd cornered a helpless bird, and he was still humming that infernal song under his breath.

"Oh, do be quiet," she said, more exasperated with herself than with him.

"Don't shout, my darling Clementine. You'll wake Miss Josephine. What would she say about you cavorting with a Hollywood man?"

Clemmie almost laughed. If he knew what Miss Josephine had already said about him he wouldn't be so insouciant.

"I'm not cavorting, I'm..." Clemmie hesitated, confused. What was she doing? Michael had one eyebrow lifted in that cocky, wicked way of his, and she was hanging out her window like some two-bit floozy, dressed in nothing but her nightgown, to boot.

She pulled back with alarm and crossed her arms over her chest. Although her gown was a perfectly respectable cotton with a sweetheart neckline, she wasn't taking any chances. Michael laughed, and then, to make matters worse, he started singing again. Now was no time for timidity, Clemmie told herself as she grabbed her robe and headed out the door. She'd have to deal with him the way she would deal with any problem boarder—with courage and firmness.

The minute she stepped into the moonlight with Michael Forrest, courage and firmness gave way to butterflies in the stomach and marshmallow legs. How was it possible that God had put so much perfection into one man? Her plans to scold him gave way to a desire to sink onto the porch steps and simply gaze at him. And that glorious smile he gave her didn't help one bit.

"You came." He left the gazebo and started toward her, stopping when he was close enough to touch.

"Of course, I came. I came to..." Her voice trailed off as he took her hand and lifted it to his lips.

"...make me feel as welcome as that grand group of people at Woody's," he finished smoothly. He could feel her hand tremble in his. Innocent. The word blazed through his mind like a comet. And that gown and robe she was wearing...white cotton, for God's sake. It made his throat ache in a way that all the black lace in the world couldn't do.

"I'm glad you came out, Clemmie." He swept his free hand to include the moonswept gazebo, the towering oaks, their leaves rustling with autumn secrets, and the night sky, ablaze with stars. "This is a setting that shouldn't be wasted. Will you sit with me in the gazebo?"

He was still holding her hand. Clemmie was surprised at how good that simple act felt. Looking up at him, she wondered why she had dreaded coming out. He was wearing a little boy look of anticipation that made her heart turn over.

"It's late and I probably shouldn't . . ."

"For me, Clemmie."

"I don't usually do this kind of thing...dressed in my nightgown and all."

He suppressed a grin. "You look perfectly respectable."

"I do?"

"Certainly." His gaze swept over her. "You don't even have any skin showing, except a small spot below your chin, right above those ruffles."

"Oh." Her free hand went up to cover her throat.

An unbearable tenderness caught at him. He reached up and covered the hand that rested on her throat. "Don't, Clemmie." Slowly he pulled her hand away. "Don't hide from me." Her eyes were luminous as he cupped her face. "Your skin is so soft in the moonlight. Let me touch it."

He brushed his fingers in butterfly-light caresses across her throat, then moved them upward to touch her cheeks. She closed her eyes and sighed.

"You like that, don't you?"

It never occurred to Clemmie to lie. "Yes. Oh, yes."

"I do, too." Michael allowed himself to prolong the magical moment long enough to memorize the exact structure of her cheekbones, the precise silky texture of her skin, the exact slant of her exotic jade eyes. *I like it all right,* he said to himself. *Too damned much.*

Abruptly he released her face, tucked her hand through his arm and hurried off toward the gazebo.

"Michael?"

"I invited you to sit in the gazebo."

If Clemmie had not been so enraptured by the gentle way he'd touched her cheeks and gazed into her eyes, she'd have noticed the gruffness of his voice, the grim set of his mouth. But she was caught up in the thrill of romance. Her mind was happily sailing ahead, planning the words she would use to invite him to the church social.

The gazebo would be the perfect place. In the moonlight it had an air of magic. Its white latticed sides gleamed like spun sugar, and night wind whispered symphonies through the arched openings.

Her white gown billowed around her as she settled onto the bench. She looked out through the lattice at the stars and smiled. She knew just how it would be. She'd say, "Michael, will you be my guest tomorrow night at the church social?" and he would flash that endearing little-boy-at-Christmastime smile and say, "I thought you'd never ask," and then they would laugh together. She loved the way he laughed, deep and rumbly and uninhibited, like thunder through the hills.

Michael gazed down at her, his longing clearly stamped on every feature. But Clemmie was too caught up in her own plans to notice. The autumn breeze sighed around them, lifting Clemmie's hair back from her face.

Stifling a curse, Michael shook his head like an old dog, which wasn't far from the way he was feeling. Protecting himself—and her—by being the cad was going to be one of the hardest things he'd ever done. But now more than ever, he had to play the role. The woman sitting in front of him was stripping away his defenses one by one. If he didn't start putting them back up, he'd soon be hopelessly lost. And then they'd both be sorry.

"Are you cold, Clemmie?" He sat down beside her and drew her smoothly into his arms. She stiffened at his sudden move, but she made no attempt to pull away. He almost wished she had; he almost wished she'd gotten up and run back into the house.

"Now that you mention it, I suppose I am." She tried to make herself relax and settle into his arms. Wasn't that the way it was ordinarily done? It had been so long she had forgotten such a simple thing as letting a man court her.

"I have a remedy for that."

He pulled her closer so that her breasts were pressed tightly against his chest. And the way he was running his hands down her arms was intimate, somehow. Wasn't it too soon for that? she wondered as she struggled for composure.

"Relax, love. I won't hurt you."

"I know that."

He felt like Jack the Ripper. *Don't,* he wanted to yell. *Don't trust me.* Instead he grimly set about his seduction.

"Has any man ever told you that you're beautiful in the moonlight?"

"No." Her answer was a small whisper, almost a sigh that stirred her warm breath against his neck. He hardened his heart.

"Then they've all been fools. You are gorgeous." He bent over her and traced his lips down the side of her cheek. "Luscious . . . delicious," he murmured, following the smooth curve of her jaw with his lips. He could feel the frantic pounding of her heart. He ignored it.

"How long since a man has kissed you, Clemmie?"

"It seems forever."

That honesty was almost his undoing.

"Then it's high time you were put back in the mainstream of life."

Clemmie shivered as his mouth seared down the side of her throat and nudged intimately into the top of her ruffles. Things were moving so fast, too fast. But, oh my, she thought, it felt so good. She figured her face must be positively glowing with the joy of it all. Did Michael feel that way, too?

She drew back to look at his face, and what she saw shocked her. He looked fierce and determined and yet. . . She studied him in the moonlight. There was something infinitely sad and moving about his eyes. Those incredible amber eyes looked shattered, as if someone had taken a sledgehammer and pounded them to pieces.

She touched his face. "Michael?"

"Oh, God. Don't look at me like that."

"Like what?"

"Don't, Clemmie."

Suddenly his mouth came down on hers with a force that took her breath away. His lips were fierce and demanding. Clemmie had never been kissed like that, even by her fiancé. She'd wanted Michael to kiss her; she really had. But she had hoped for tenderness and maybe a little controlled passion, not this heady assault that made her weak. Or had she?

Feelings she'd never known coursed through her as Michael's tongue found its way between her lips and delved intimately into her mouth. She experienced something that was almost like rebirth. Each spring she'd watched the greening of the earth. She'd seen the trees sprouting fresh leaves and tiny buds; she'd witnessed the transforming of blossoms into fruit. In Michael's arms she felt as if she were greening. And it was glorious.

She heard him groan, or was it herself? It didn't matter. Nothing seemed to matter right now except savoring this moment. She leaned into Michael's chest, offering herself to him with complete trust.

Abruptly he pulled away and gazed down at her. "You're so damned innocent."

The anguish in his voice confused her. "I know I'm not very practiced at this sort of thing..."

"Hush, Clemmie." He swept her back into his arms and pressed her so close she could feel every ragged breath he took. "Please, don't do this."

"Michael." Her voice was muffled against his shirt. "I don't know what I'm doing wrong."

"Nothing." His hands spanned her narrow waist, and he put her away from him almost roughly. "There's nothing wrong with you, Clemmie, except that you're too damned trusting."

"But Michael, we're friends."

"You don't even know me." He reached out and gripped her shoulders. "God, Clemmie. How do you know those stories you read about me aren't true? How do you know I won't take advantage of you out here in the dark?"

Clemmie didn't understand what had gone wrong. Michael had been kissing her, and then he'd pushed her away. Somehow that didn't seem right. She was certain that if she'd had more experience she'd know exactly how to deal with the situation. But all she had was pride.

Pressing her hands together in her lap to hold them steady, she lifted her chin and looked him straight in the eye. "I'm thirty years old, Michael. I can take care of myself."

His smile was bittersweet. "Can you, Clemmie?" He studied her for a long moment, those golden eyes seeming to penetrate right through her. She'd be willing to bet that he knew she was shaking inside.

She lifted her chin a fraction higher. "Yes, I can."

He chuckled, but it wasn't a sound of mirth. To Clemmie's heightened senses, it was almost a sound of sadness.

"Do you know how easy it would be for me?" His face became fierce as he leaned toward her and put one hand on her throat. The feather-light touch made her shiver. His hand moved down and popped open the top button on her cotton robe. A surprised gasp escaped her lips, but she made herself sit very still. She had to prove to him that she was no babe in the woods.

He opened the second button. "Have you any idea how many women I've undressed, Clemmie? How many women I've had?" His hands worked the third button open, then drew the robe apart. She felt the cool rush of night air on her chest. It made her shiver. Or was it the look in Michael's eyes that made her shiver? They were glowing as if candles had been lit in their center.

"Afraid, Clemmie?"

"No."

"You should be."

He placed one hand on her chest, pressing his palm warmly over the spot where her heart beat, spreading his fingers wide so he could cover the entire expanse of flesh left bare by the top of her gown.

Neither of them spoke. In the distance an owl sounded its mournful message, and around them the night breeze whispered its secrets in a hushed voice.

Michael was the first to break the silence. "I could take you right now, in this gazebo." His hand began to make small circles on her bare chest. "I could peel away all those innocent layers of white cotton until I had you naked in my arms."

Clemmie wet her dry lips. "I know that," she whispered.

"Then why in the hell aren't you running?" Michael jerked his hand off her chest and pulled her robe back together. "Don't give yourself to me, Clemmie. You deserve better." His hands fumbled as he fastened the buttons.

"Michael." She put her hands over his. "I like you. I don't mind . . ." She hesitated. What was it she could say to this man to wipe away that fierce scowl? What could she do to bring back the laughter and the songs? Never mind the kiss.

"Please, Michael." Ignoring her soft plea, he continued to work angrily at the buttons. Clemmie's frustration boiled over. "Stop that."

He pulled back, one eyebrow quirked upward.

"I know what I want, Michael." She stood up and stepped back so she could have the advantage of looking down at him. "I'm a grown woman, and if I want to throw myself at your feet, I will. And I don't need you or anybody else to tell me what I should do."

"Bravo, Clemmie." He clapped his hands, and the sound was hollow in the night stillness of the gazebo. "And what is it you want?" Standing up, he pulled her against his chest. "This?" He pressed his hands over her hips, molding them intimately against his own. "And this?" His hands abruptly left her hips and moved up to cradle her breasts.

He covered her mouth once more. When he finally pulled back, she thought her knees would buckle. Putting her hand over her lips, she stared at him.

"Go to the house, Clemmie." Michael stepped back and leaned against the side of the gazebo. His face was hidden in the darkness, but his voice was cold and harsh. "You're out of your league with me."

Clemmie wanted to deny his words. She wanted to touch his face and soothe away the pain she sensed was there. But her lips felt bruised and her knees felt shaky. She decided to leave while she still could.

"Good night, Michael."

She waited a half second for his reply, but none came. Turning slowly, she left the gazebo and started back toward the house.

Michael didn't come down to breakfast the next morning.

Clemmie sat at the head of the dining room table, serving the plantation breakfast to Miss Josephine and Harvey and trying not to look disappointed that her Hollywood boarder was nowhere in sight.

"Pass me another biscuit, Clementine," Miss Josephine shouted. "You look a mite peaked today."

Clemmie picked up the basket of hot biscuits and handed it to her. "It must be the weather."

Josephine tore off a piece of biscuit and popped it into her mouth. "No," she yelled, "they're not light as a feather, but they are mighty tasty."

At the other end of the table, Harvey snickered. Clementine was too tired to whisper "be nice to her" as she usually did. On the pretext of refilling the coffee server, she left the dining room and went into the kitchen. As she passed the stairs, she stopped, listening for sounds of Michael Forrest. There was nothing except silence.

He was probably in his bed right this very minute, she told herself, sleeping as if nothing had happened in the gazebo last night. And here she was, standing in the hallway like an idiot, still mooning over the way his lips had felt on hers, the way his hands had made her feel hot all over. She even felt hot now, just thinking about it.

She heard a creak on the staircase that made her jump, but it was only the old house shifting on its tired foundation. Relieved that the sound hadn't been Michael, that he hadn't caught her spying up the stairs, she hurried to the kitchen; then she forgot why she had come. Turning around in a helpless circle, she spotted a jar of blackberry jelly. She picked it up and carried it back to the dining room.

"Look what I've found to go with the biscuits," she announced with forced cheer as she put the jelly on the table. "I made it last year when the berries were ripe."

"I thought you went for coffee." Harvey adjusted his glasses that were always sliding down his nose, and smiled at her.

Clemmie wanted to scream. Never had the burden of being an innkeeper been so great. On a day when she wanted to bury herself under the covers, she had to play the hostess to a man whose smile made him look like a horse and an old woman wearing a dead corsage.

"I guess I forgot," she snapped, then she was immediately ashamed of herself. She didn't know what was wrong with her. She'd never had unkind thoughts about Harvey and Miss Josephine. She loved them.

"I'm sorry. I didn't sleep well last night, and I guess I'm peevish."

"No problem," Harvey said as he helped himself to the jelly. "Who needs coffee when they can have fresh jelly?"

"Did you say Shelly's back?" Josephine turned to Clemmie, a smear of butter clinging to her chin. "I thought she was still in St. Louis."

Clemmie left her chair and bent over the old lady, gently wiping away the butter. "No, dear, Shelly's not back. But she will be soon."

"Went to the moon, you say? I *did* think it was St. Louis."

"St. Louis," Harvey shouted. "They're still in St. Louis."

"Good." Josephine smiled. "I hope they stay there so I can eat their biscuits."

"Thanks, Harvey." Clemmie gave him a grateful smile. He could be very nice when he wanted to be, she thought. And he really didn't look so much like a horse. More like a rabbit, with his big front teeth. A *nice* rabbit, she amended.

"You're welcome, Clemmie." He pushed back his chair and stood up. "Will you be at the church social tonight?"

"Why...yes."

"Good." He stood uncertainly, as if he wanted to say more, then he started toward the door, calling over his shoulder, "Maybe I'll see you there."

Clemmie watched him leave, dependable Harvey with his loose-jointed scarecrow walk and his flyaway baby bird hair. A sudden vision of Michael in the moonlight came to her. She could see him as clearly as if he were sitting in one of her dining room chairs. Unconsciously she put her hand over her heart, right on the spot he'd touched last night. Michael Forrest was the man she wanted to see at the church social. He was the man she wanted to bid on her box, the man she wanted to share her meal with. Instead she had Harvey.

Clemmie sighed. At least Harvey wouldn't try to seduce her in the gazebo.

"Are you going with me to the church social tonight?" she shouted in Josephine's ear.

"Tonight?"

"That's right." Clemmie was relieved that for once Miss Josephine had heard what she'd said. As she helped the old lady from the chair she thought of the gazebo. The strange thing was that she'd wanted to be seduced in the gazebo.

"Oh, my no." Miss Josephine put a thin hand on Clemmie's arm. "Don't you know? Junior always pays me a visit on Saturday night." She smiled archly up at the young woman who was more like a daughter to her than a landlady. "It's our night to howl."

Clemmie patted Josephine's hand. "Then you'll want to put on your Sunday best. This evening before I leave for the church I'll help you change your dress."

"My sentiments exactly. That Harvey does make a mess. And just listen to that racket." Josephine pressed one hand over her ear to shut out the noise of Harvey's practice. "I wish he'd play something nice like the piccolo."

The deep brassy notes of the tuba drifted up the stairs as Clemmie helped Miss Josephine to her room. Another typical Saturday at the boarding house. When she passed Michael's closed door, she amended that last thought. The day wasn't typical at all, for Michael Forrest was behind that closed door, sleeping in the big brass bed.

Clemmie wondered what it would be like to be in that bed with him. She guessed she'd never know. After last night it was perfectly obvious that he preferred women who were sophisticated and experienced.

It was just as well. She'd never really believed there could be anything between them except a few torrid kisses in the gazebo. And he'd certainly given her that. It was a memory that would last a lifetime.

When she left Miss Josephine and went back downstairs, she was smiling.

The sound of the tuba awakened Michael.

He rolled over and glimpsed the sunlight shining on the brass footboard of the bed. For a moment he was disoriented, then it all came back to him—last night in the gazebo, Clemmie in her innocent white cotton gown.

"Damn." He jerked the covers back and sat up. The clock on the bedside table said eight. He'd missed his morning jog; he'd missed breakfast; he'd gotten behind with all the work he'd planned. And all because he'd let a woman with exotic eyes and a vamp's mouth get under his skin.

He wouldn't let that happen today, he vowed as he padded naked across the hardwood floor to the bathroom. He'd keep out of her way. Hell, he'd even get out of Peppertown, the sooner the better. It might be cowardly, but there was only so much sweetness a man could stand.

Michael showered and dressed quickly, then hurried down the stairs, intent on getting out of the house and completing his business so he could get back to Hollywood. The sound of Clemmie's singing stopped him. Her clear, true voice riveted him to the staircase. He tensed, as if he had been hit with high-voltage electricity. The music drifted from the kitchen, settling around him like a benediction and stirring ancient memories—Grandmother Forrest, bending over a bit of needlework, singing one of her favorite hymns, "Rock of Ages," the song Clemmie was singing now.

He couldn't have been more than three or four years old when Grandmother Forrest had first come to visit with them. His mother had been on location in Greece, and his father had had a once-in-a-lifetime attack of conscience and decided that he'd be a family man. And so Grandmother Forrest, who had seen Michael only once, the day he was born, had come from Ohio for a visit.

Michael remembered that she'd smelled like gingerbread and violets. And she was always singing. The week she'd stayed with them had been the happiest of his life. She'd read bedtime stories and baked gingerbread boys and had even taught him how to throw a curve ball. Granny, as she'd insisted on being called, had gotten the map and pointed out Ohio. She'd promised that when he was old enough, he could come and spend summers with her on her farm.

It was a promise she never kept. Two years after her visit, she'd died.

Shaking himself out of his reverie, Michael descended the stairs and headed for the front door. In the hallway, he stopped. The unmistakable aroma of gingerbread drifted from the kitchen.

Michael was overcome with a sense of déjà vu. He could no more have passed by that kitchen than he could have denied his own name.

Retracing his steps, he walked to the kitchen and leaned against the door frame. Clemmie was standing at the kitchen cabinet, a smudge of flour on her cheek, cutting out gingerbread boys and still singing. The sight of her made Michael feel warm all over.

"Is that gingerbread I smell?"

Clemmie's song came to an abrupt halt. One hand came up to her face, spreading another streak of flour on her cheek. "You startled me."

"I'm sorry. I didn't mean to."

"That's all right. Boarders come and go. I shouldn't have been startled." She smiled, a beautiful shy curving of her berry red lips. "I guess my mind was somewhere else." *In the gazebo,* she added to herself.

"Mine was, too." *In the moonlight with you in my arms,* he thought.

"It was?"

"Yes. Your singing reminded me of my grandmother. She used to make gingerbread."

"This is for my brothers. They love gingerbread. I'm going to package it up and mail it to them at college."

"I wish I had a sister like you." He lingered in the doorway, reluctant to leave and yet daring not stay. "About last night, Clemmie . . ."

"Oh." Clemmie put her hand to her throat, dappling it with flour.

Michael fought the urge to cross the room and kiss those smudges away. "Damn!"

"What?"

"Nothing. I just remembered that I'm late for an appointment."

Michael whirled around and strode down the hallway. Clemmie heard the front door bang shut behind him.

"Oh." She reached blindly for a kitchen chair and sat down. Goodness gracious, she thought. She could never seem to handle these meetings with Michael. What she should have said was, "Hello, there, Michael. Do you want some gingerbread?" And he would have said, "Of course." Then he'd have sat at the kitchen table and they could have chatted like friends. Finally, at just the right moment, she could have said, "The church social is tonight. Won't you be my guest?" And he would have said, "I was hoping you'd ask."

Why couldn't things come out the way she planned them in her head?

Clemmie sat a moment longer in her straight-back kitchen chair, listening to the tick of the clock on the wall and smelling the pungent aroma of cinnamon. Time was marching steadily on, and she had nothing for company except gingerbread boys. Of course, she reasoned, Michael would be going back to Hollywood soon, and she'd still have her brothers and her boarders and her friends and her lovely old house in a wonderful old town. How silly of her to sit brooding.

Picking up the song where she'd left off, Clemmie went back to her baking.

Chapter Five

Michael spent all of Saturday scouting locations and getting permission from landowners to bring in his movie crew. He pushed himself to the limit, squeezing at least three days' work into one. Only when it was too dark to see did he allow himself to return to Brady's Boarding House.

The Victorian house looked peaceful in the early evening, as if it welcomed the respite from a day's activities. Set back among the fall-dressed trees, it looked warm and inviting. As Michael parked his rental car he thought about the place he called home. It was an adobe mansion filled with tile and marble, and it had about as much warmth as his mother's cold heart.

Before Michael had met Clemmie, a house had been merely a house to him, a place to sleep and sometimes eat. Now he found himself loitering in the front yard, reflecting on the qualities that made a house a home—the smell of gingerbread baking, the sound of laughter in the halls, the presence of a woman with a gift for tenderness.

Michael impatiently shook his head. The next thing he knew, he'd be looking at property to buy. In this little cow town, for God's sake. If he didn't get his mind off Clemmie, he'd go as soft as a down pillow.

Giving a snort of disgust, he mounted the front porch steps and went into the house.

"Is that you, Junior?" Miss Josephine's voice quavered, stopping him in the hallway.

"No. I'm not Junior."

"Well, don't just stand there, Junior." Miss Josephine appeared in a doorway to his right. Dressed in lavender chiffon and wearing a rhinestone tiara, she looked like an aging silent screen actress. Michael had glimpsed her as he'd passed her room upstairs, and he knew from last night when she'd leaned out the window that she was hard of hearing. But he'd never seen her close up. She had a magnetism, that quality called charisma, that drew him to her. "Come on in the parlor so we can have a drink together."

Intrigued, he followed her into the room she called the parlor. It looked like a set from the movie *Arsenic and Old Lace*. Marble-topped tables, silk brocade chairs, and a Duncan Phyfe sofa were arranged in a cozy grouping in front of the fireplace. There were lace curtains at the window and real roses in a vase on an ancient spinet.

Miss Josephine sat on the sofa and patted a spot beside her. "Sit here, Junior. I want to feast my eyes on you."

"Miss Josephine..." He'd started to tell her that he wasn't Junior when she put her hand over his lips. It felt like a piece of old parchment.

"Shush, young man. I know you're not Junior. You're that scandalous Hollywood man who's come to seduce us all." Reaching for the decanter of wine, she chuckled. "Being old has its advantages, you know. I can get by with most anything." She poured two glasses and handed one to him.

"Thank you." He took a sip and was shocked at the potency of the drink.

"Knocked your pants off, didn't it?" Miss Josephine laughed. "Blackberry wine. I talked Clemmie into making it last summer."

He leaned close and shouted so she could hear him. "It's potent. But good."

"The same way I like my men, potent and good." Miss Josephine tilted her head and arched one eyebrow at him. "Do I shock you, young man?"

"No. You enchant me."

He couldn't tell whether or not she'd understood. Instead of replying, she leaned back against the sofa and closed her eyes. If it weren't for the smile on her face, he'd have been alarmed. Finally she opened her eyes and winked at him.

"You say mighty pretty words in a mighty pretty voice."

Lifting her free hand, he bent over and kissed it. "Pretty words for a charming lady."

"They're wasted on me. There's somebody else in this house you should be saying them to." She chuckled at the shocked expression on his face. "I saw you and Clemmie in the gazebo last night. I was spying."

"She's merely a passing fancy."

"I'd get antsy, too, about what she's doing tonight."

"It's no concern of mine." He drank his wine, trying to look totally bored with the subject of Clemmie.

"She's down yonder at the church. Probably got some pious bore bidding on her supper box right now. He'll take her out under the trees and tell her how great her fried chicken is before he tries to get under her skirts."

Michael put his glass on the marble-topped table with such force it threatened to shatter. The thought of Clemmie in the clutches of some bumbling maniac made his blood boil.

"Miss Josephine, I hope to hell you can hear me, because a man doesn't like to make a fool of himself more than once. Where is that damned church?"

Miss Josephine clapped her hands with glee. "I *do* love to meddle." Getting a paper and pencil from the piano bench, she drew a map.

"Her box is pink with a bright blue ribbon," she said as she handed him the map and waved him goodbye. Then she sat back on the sofa, waiting for her dear departed Junior Wade.

Michael swore all the way to the church. He cursed the balky rental car, blackened the reputations of all the local swains, and spared a few scathing words for himself. By the time he got to the church he was as nervous as a bridegroom. He sat in the car, glaring at the massive front doors and thinking of a million reasons why he shouldn't go inside. In the end, there was one reason why he did—Clemmie.

Sneaking around had never been his style, so when he made his entrance it was a grand one. He strode boldly down the center aisle of the small white-framed church toward the front pew. Heads turned and a flutter of whisperings accompanied his march down the aisle.

Clemmie was directly in front of him, sitting in the choir loft, dressed in a blue shirtwaist that made her look like a sixteen-year-old school girl. All she needed was a ponytail to make the image complete. When she saw him, her eyes widened and her cheeks got pink.

Michael winked. Her cheeks got even brighter. He stared at her for so long he began to feel self-conscious and a bit foolish. But then, he supposed that's how someone on a fool's errand should feel—foolish.

At the pulpit, the minister cleared his throat. "As I was saying...here's a lovely box." He held a red gingham box aloft. "It's heavy, too. Just waiting for some hungry man to put in his bid."

The bidding was lively and good-natured, but Michael paid scant attention. He was too busy trying to see if he could spot Clemmie's box among those stacked beside the minister. Unfortunately the altar rail got in the way.

Finally a young man with a cowlick paid ten dollars for the gingham box.

The minister gave his congregation a smile, glistening with sweat and earnestness. "That's a wonderful start. Remember now, it's all for a good cause. Let's see if we can't keep that pace up with our second box."

That meant that Clemmie's box was still waiting to be sold. Michael felt a sense of relief that was out of proportion to the situation. He settled back on the hard pew and gazed at Clemmie as the minister auctioned off the gold-wrapped box. The contrast between the exotic appeal of her face and the prim message of her white-collared dress twisted Michael's gut. It had been a long time since he'd been inside a church, but he knew his thoughts were not appropriate. Definitely not religious and lofty.

He dragged his gaze away from Clemmie as the minister held high a pink box tied with a blue ribbon.

From the back pew, a voice piped up, "I bid two dollars."

Oblivious of the whispers around him, Michael turned to locate the bidder. It was Harvey, the downstairs boarder, the one who had awakened him with that damned tuba this morning. He'd met him briefly in the hallway when Harvey had stuck his head around the doorway as Michael stomped away from Clemmie and her gingerbread.

"Twenty," Michael said, pinning Harvey to his seat with a fierce scowl.

"Twenty-one." The voice came from Michael's right. He had to swivel all the way around in order to find the man who was bidding—a slicked-up character who looked as if he couldn't be trusted with the Mafia let alone with Clemmie.

"Fifty," Michael roared.

The congregation gave a collective gasp that seemed to hang in the air like pollution before it drifted back down on a sigh.

The minister got so excited he pounded on the pulpit. "Going once, going twice..."

"Fifty-five." The voice almost squeaked with excitement. Harvey, again.

Michael quickly upped the ante. "One hundred."

A hush came over the crowd. Nobody had ever bid more than twenty-five dollars at one of these box socials, even if the money did go to a good cause. People in the back craned their necks to get a better view of the stranger in their midst.

Even the minister was too surprised to say anything.

Suddenly the stillness was broken by another bid. "One twenty-five."

It was the shifty maniac on Michael's right again. Michael shot him a murderous glance.

Up front, the minister, recovering from the shock and happily anticipating the large amount of money that would go into the mission fund, sang out, "Going once, going twice, sol—"

Michael's voice cut in as cold and hard as a steel blade. "One thousand."

Bedlam broke loose. A woman in the back of the church fainted; the teenagers broke into a cheer; an old codger in overalls pounded the pew and yelled, "Well, hallelujah and glory be."

In the midst of the uproar, Michael looked at Clemmie. Her face was as pink as the sugar roses on her birthday cake, but she was smiling. He winked at her, then slouched back into his seat as if what he had done was no big deal, certainly not to him. The bidding was over; he knew that. He could relax now for no man would get his clutches on Clemmie tonight. Hell, he could even pay his one thousand dollars and leave if he wanted to.

He glanced at Clemmie again. The tip of her tongue came out and wet her lips. Michael decided he'd stay, after all. He had to eat, didn't he? He reached into his pocket and pulled out his checkbook, but it wasn't a contribution to missions he was thinking about: it was Clemmie's sweet smile.

The last boxes were bid off, but they were anticlimactic. The best show was over.

"Ladies and gentlemen, thank you for your generous support of our missions," the minister said. "Without further ado, let the fun begin. The fellowship hall is open for those who want to eat there. There are picnic tables out back for those who can stand the cool night air. And now—" he paused dramatically, then held up the red gingham box "—claim your boxes and claim your date for the evening."

Michael was the last to claim his box. In a great show of nonchalance, he picked it up and looked across the heads of the crowd at Clemmie as she made her way slowly toward him. When she arrived, she was breathless. His nonchalance vanished.

"Clemmie."

"Michael."

For a moment they looked at each other as if they were the only two people in the room. Finally, Clemmie broke the spell.

"What you did tonight was very generous."

"No, Clemmie. Merely selfish."

"How could paying one thousand dollars for charity be selfish?"

"I didn't pay it for charity. I paid it so no other man could get his hands on you."

Behind them, a couple of matrons with plasticlike hairdos and too much makeup gasped.

Clemmie pressed her hands together and tried to act as if her heart weren't climbing out of her chest. "Michael, I do believe you're a tease—like my brothers."

"My thoughts right now are hardly brotherly." He took her elbow and steered her toward the door. "Let's get out of here before I make a complete fool of myself."

"You could never do that."

"I already have."

They were silent, each lost in thought as they stepped into the cool evening air. Down the sidewalk, the lights of the fellowship hall shot beacons into the darkness.

"Do you want to eat inside, Michael?"

"No. I want you as far away from that conniving maniac as I can get."

"Who?"

"That slick number who kept bidding on your box. Who is he?"

"Harvey?"

"Not Harvey. That man with the greedy eyes and sleazy grin who couldn't wait to get you alone in the dark."

"Why, that was only Mr. Clark."

"Mister? You call a man who was willing to pay over a hundred dollars for an evening in your company *mister*?"

"Everybody does. He's the postman."

"I don't care if he's Santa Claus. He had no business trying to take advantage of an innocent woman."

The amusement that had been bubbling up in Clemmie spilled over. Leaning against a pine tree, she gave vent to the hearty laughter.

Michael didn't see a damned thing funny about the situation, except perhaps that he had set out to rescue Clemmie in the first place. A battle-scarred knight in tarnished armor had gone charging up the church steps to deliver her from the clutches of the postman. He had no business being there. If it hadn't been for that silvery patch of moonlight on Clemmie's throat he would have turned tail and run. As it was, all he could do was ram his fists into his pants pocket and ache.

Suddenly the laughter stopped. Clemmie reached up and touched his cheek. "Don't look so fierce, Michael."

The caress was butterfly soft, but it branded him. "Don't." He jerked his head back. "Don't play with fire, Clemmie."

"Michael . . ."

"Why in the hell was the postman bidding on your box anyway? Why didn't he pick on some other innocent woman?"

Clemmie was stunned by Michael's strange behavior. And she was beginning to lose patience. It was something she didn't do very often because she couldn't afford not to be in control, but Michael Forrest had an uncanny knack for getting under her skin.

"What difference does it make to you, Michael? What do you care?"

"Call it a latent streak of nobility. Call it any damned thing you want to. I don't want to see any man take advantage of you."

"Mr. Clark would never try to take advantage of me. And he's certainly never kissed me in the gazebo the way you did."

"Good."

"Don't look so smug. Mr. Clark can be quite charming. In fact, the couple of times we've gone out he's held my hand and . . . he has his ways."

He grabbed her shoulders and hauled her close. "What do you mean, he has his ways?"

"Be quiet. They'll hear you clear at the church."

"I don't care if they hear me in Hong Kong. I want to know what Mr. Clark did besides hold your hand."

In spite of the way her heart was hammering, Clemmie gathered her courage. She thrust her face right into his and glowered. "You have no right to know."

"I'm making it my right." He released one of her shoulders and caught her face. "Tell me, Clemmie. Did he try to seduce you?"

"St. Peter's britches!"

"Did he?"

She struggled, but it was no use. She was no match for Michael. "You're the only one who has ever tried to seduce me. Only you, Michael." Her face flamed and his expression softened. "Are you satisfied? Now will you let me go?"

He held her a moment longer, caressing her face with his hands, calling himself a million kinds of fool. At last he spoke. "I'm sorry, Clemmie." Releasing her, he stepped back into the shadow of the pine. "I had no right to question you."

"It's okay, Michael." She placed her hand on his arm.

But it was not okay, he told himself. What he'd done was rude and overbearing, and her quick forgiveness made matters worse. Nothing about this evening was the way it should be. The pleasant warmth that seeped through him at her touch was not all right. The strange urge to pull Clemmie into his arms and hold her, merely hold her, was dangerous.

Ah, but her touch felt so good that he almost gave in. Then the voice of reason spoke to him. Hadn't he known enough heartache in his lifetime? Hadn't he learned from the lessons of the past? No matter how women were packaged—sweet and innocent like Clemmie or stunningly erotic like Hubbard—they always spelled trouble.

He brushed her hands away and stepped back. Clemmie looked so vulnerable in her prim little dress. So confused. So heart-breakingly innocent. He'd already broken all the rules with her, but no more, he vowed.

He'd not embarrass her further by leaving her alone with her dinner box, but neither would he act like some demented swain.

"I paid a thousand dollars to see what's in that box. Let's eat." He pulled off his coat.

"Here?"

"Yes. If you don't mind I'd rather not socialize with the church crowd tonight." He spread his coat on the pine needles covering the ground. "You can sit here."

A wave of tenderness washed over Clemmie. Michael's afraid, she thought. And in his own way, vulnerable. He didn't want anyone to discover he wasn't the tough guy he pretended to be.

She sat down on his coat and watched him squat beside the dinner box. When he lifted the lid, the smell of fresh gingerbread wafted up to them. The grin of delight on his face made her feel good. A man's smile hadn't made her feel that way in a long, long time. Since Johnny Lackey. The knowledge coursed through her like new wine.

"You brought gingerbread."

"Yes. I hoped you would come."

"Why, Clemmie?"

"Because I like you, Michael."

"I've done nothing to deserve your regard." He studied her in silence, taking secret delight in the way the moonlight kissed her skin, marveling at the tenderness he felt for this innocent, exotic woman. Finally he tore his gaze away from her, lifted the gingerbread boy out of the box and deliberately bit off its head. Next he ate the arms and legs. He had to prove there was no significance in the gingerbread boy. When only the body was left, he said, "And I don't plan to do anything to deserve your regard. So beware, my darling Clementine."

"When my brothers are troubled, they deliberately do something to make me believe they are bold and brash and carefree. What's troubling you, Michael? Perhaps I can help."

Since his grandmother, no one had cared what was troubling Michael. For a moment he was tempted to confide in Clemmie, then he regained his senses. Tender traps were the worst of all.

Laughing, he reached into the box and brought out a fried chicken leg. "I'm no longer that little boy who could be won over by his grandmother's gingerbread." He bit into the chicken almost savagely. "I suppose in your profession you are tempted to practice amateur psychology."

"Sometimes I do listen to my boarder's problems. But I don't call it psychology: I call it friendship."

He felt lower than a grubworm. Affecting a debonair smile, he tweaked her cheek. "Give me inches and I take miles, offer me your friendship and I take your body, too."

"Well..." Hesitating, Clemmie looked deep into his eyes. Then, taking a deep breath, she plunged ahead, "...that might not be such a bad thing."

Michael tossed the fried chicken into the box and grabbed her shoulders. "Listen to me. You can't go around offering yourself to men, especially not men like me. What in the hell is the matter with you?"

"I'm thirty."

"What does that have to do with anything?"

"Romance is passing me by, Michael."

"A tumble in bed with a stranger is not romance."

"Well, it's not canned pickles, either."

"Canned pickles?"

"And canned tomatoes, and canned green beans and canned squash. Sometimes I feel as though I'm putting little bits of myself into jars to store on the pantry shelf. I don't want to sit on the shelf forever."

At that moment Michael wished he were a knight in shining armor instead of a tarnished, jaded Don Juan.

Leaning down, he tenderly kissed her cheek. "You won't, Clemmie. Someday the right man is going to come along and discover what a treasure you are. Until then—" his eyes held hers for a moment, then he released her "—let's eat our fried chicken."

Michael ate his dinner as quickly as possible while deftly steering the conversation away from personal things. They talked of politics and music and theater. Clemmie accepted the situation with grace and wit and charm. When he bid her goodbye, patted her on the cheek and thanked her for the dinner, she was smiling.

Her smile haunted him all the way back to Brady's Boarding House. After parking the car under the pines, he gripped the steering wheel and sat staring at the house. Clemmie would be back soon, and he knew he couldn't spend another night in the same house with her. That was too much temptation for any man to bear.

With a muttered curse he started the car and headed west on Highway 78 toward Tupelo. There was certain to be a good piano bar where he could listen to the blues and forget. Hell, in a city that size he'd probably even have his choice of night spots. If he tried hard enough he could block Clemmie from his mind with a couple of glasses of wine and plenty of heartbreaking blues, then he'd check into a motel.

Michael had forgotten his coat. Probably because she'd been sitting on it, Clemmie thought as she picked it up and brushed the pine needles away.

"Hi, Clemmie. Have a nice dinner?"

"Hello, Harvey." She folded the coat carefully and draped it over her arm. "Yes, we did. Did you? I noticed you bought Earnestine's box."

"Yeah." Harvey scuffed his shoes among the leaves. "About that man who bought your box..."

"Michael Forrest?"

"Isn't he that boarder, the one Miss Josephine says was involved in all that scandal?"

"He's a very fine man, Harvey. You shouldn't pay any attention to those gossip sheets."

"I was just worried about you, that's all. A man like that, from Hollywood...you never know what will happen."

St. Peter's britches, she thought. Why did everybody insist on treating her like somebody's kid sister? She wished something *would* happen.

Sighing, she patted Harvey's arm. "Don't worry about me, Harvey. Nobody's going to sweep me off my feet and carry me to Hollywood. That happens only in the movies." She picked up the dinner box. "Are you headed back to the boarding house?"

"Sure."

"How about a rousing game of checkers when we get back?"

"Great!"

The first thing Clemmie did when she got back to the boarding house was hang Michael's coat; then she helped Miss Josephine up to bed. While the old lady regaled her with stories of her evening with Junior Wade, Clemmie thought of Michael's coat. She could have put it in his room, of course, and he'd find it when he came home. But that seemed too impersonal and uncaring. Especially since he'd spent a thousand dollars on a box of fried chicken and gingerbread boys. No, she decided, she'd take the coat to him personally. It was the least she could do.

She tucked Miss Josephine into bed and went back down the stairs, detouring by her room to make sure she'd hung Michael's coat so it wouldn't get wrinkled. There it was, in the closet, right where she'd put it. She brushed her hand down one sleeve, imagining what she would say when she returned it to him.

"Here's you coat, Michael." No, that wasn't quite right. "Thank you for a lovely evening, Michael. And thank you for letting me use your coat." That was better. Of course, he'd say, "It was my pleasure, Clemmie," and then she'd say, "There's a wonderful concert at the ICC campus next week. I'd like you to be my guest . . . to show my appreciation for the church social." And he'd say—

"Are you coming, Clemmie?" Harvey's voice, calling from the parlor, broke into her reverie.

"Yes, Harvey." Her hand lingered on the coat a moment longer, then she went into the parlor for a lively game of checkers.

The next morning, as soon as breakfast was over, Clemmie hurried up the stairs with Michael's coat. She tapped on his door and waited for an answer. When there was none, she knocked again, louder this time. Still no answer.

He must still be sleeping. She had no idea what time he'd come home last night. She and Harvey had played checkers until midnight, and although she'd lain awake an hour or two after she'd gone to bed she hadn't heard Michael's car come in. He'd probably driven to Fulton or over to Tupelo and found a sophisticated woman, someone who would know more about seduction than to call it canned pickles. Her face burned at the memory.

Maybe she should simply hang the coat on the doorknob and leave.

She had the coat halfway to the doorknob when she caught a whiff of Michael's after-shave clinging to the wool fibers. Closing her eyes, she inhaled the clean spicy scent. She decided that leaving the coat on the doorknob would be cowardly. And foolish. After all, how many opportunities would she have to be in Michael's company? She didn't want to miss a single one of them.

Draping the coat over her arm, she went back downstairs to dress for church. Still holding Michael's coat, she put a recording of her favorite Verdi opera, *La Traviata*, in the tape player. As the magnificent music filled the bedroom, she held the coat like an imaginary partner and waltzed across the room, humming the melody under her breath.

She was foolishly breathless when she reached the closet.

Affecting a deep voice, she said, "You dance so divinely, Miss Brady."

"Thank you, Mr. Forrest." She bowed to the coat, then flushed and laughing, she hung it in the closet.

Still humming, she pulled off her denim skirt and blouse and reached for her blue shirtwaist dress, the one she'd worn last night. It was halfway off the hanger before she changed her mind. She knew she couldn't compete with Hollywood women, but why be prim and proper when she was a regular hoyden inside? Yes, she admitted to herself, hoyden.

Since Michael had kissed her in the gazebo, nothing had been the same. She'd always fallen into bed and slept the night through, flat on her back, her hands folded over her chest, hardly wrinkling the covers. Now she tossed and turned, her body filled with longing and her mind filled with romantic dreams.

Deciding to look a little reckless today, she reached for her nice black wool skirt and bright red turtleneck sweater. The soaring voices of Violetta and Alfredo seemed to applaud her decision.

She was pulling her sweater off the hanger when another voice made her whirl around.

"You're a vision of loveliness."

Michael was leaning against her doorway, his tie unknotted and his wrinkled shirt unbuttoned to the waist. His eyes were bloodshot from too little sleep, and his face was shadowed with a day's growth of beard.

She thought he was the most magnificent man she'd ever seen. Her face flushed hot and she made a small murmuring sound, like a hummingbird who has sucked too much nectar.

"I knocked," he said, nodding toward the tape player. "I guess you didn't hear."

"I get carried away with opera." Suddenly Clemmie became aware of her attire. She moved her arms across her chest and spread her hands over her bare shoulders. "You can't come in here. I'm not dressed."

"An enticement rather than a deterrent, my darling."

Michael still lounged in the doorway, his eyes burning over her silk-clad body. The intensity of his gaze raised a pleasant heat that started in the middle of Clemmie's chest and radiated outward. Her entire body felt sensitized. Her slip seemed to caress her, almost as if Michael's hands were on her, moving the silk against her breasts, pressing it against her flat stomach, rubbing it against her thighs.

"Harvey's room is next door, and Miss Josephine is upstairs," she said.

"Unlocked doors can be dangerous." Without taking his gaze from her, he stepped into the room and shut the door. "Is that better?"

Clemmie took a deep, shaky breath. "Yes. A little."

"Are you afraid of me, my darling?"

Her hands squeezed her shoulders. "No."

"You should be." His gaze traveled over her, but he made no move away from the door.

"Why?"

"Because you have something I want." He advanced slowly toward her. "And I usually take what I want."

Clemmie's breathing quickened so that she couldn't speak, couldn't move. Nor could she tear her eyes away from Michael's. That compelling golden gaze held her captive as he crossed the room. When he was only inches from her, he stopped. Although he wasn't touching her, she felt the full imprint of his body. The heat from his body almost reached out and seared her.

"Oh." The small sound, half-sigh, half-whisper, escaped her lips.

"Don't cover yourself, Clemmie." Michael reached up and gently pulled her hands away from her shoulders. "I want to look at you." With the tip of his index finger, he traced across her cheek and down her throat until he found her pulse point. "Your skin is soft...so very soft." He stood very still, watching her, his fingertips pressing lightly on the throbbing pulse.

Clemmie's senses were heightened so that every tiny detail was etched forever in her memory. She catalogued the cadence of Michael's harsh breathing, the exact pattern of the shadowy beard on his face, the amber fire that lit his eyes, his sensual lower lip. Her gaze slid down to his chest. A path of morning sunlight from the window glowed on the fine mat of golden hair, making it look incandescent. And irresistible. Recklessly she reached out. Only inches from that shining mat of chest hair, her hand stopped, trembled.

"Touch me, Clemmie."

When she hesitated, Michael took her hand and pressed it against his chest.

"Do you like that?" he asked

"Yes."

He guided her hand in a circle.

"It's softer than I imagined," she said.

He made a deep-throated sound that was part laughter, part agony. Her fingers curled around the hair and tugged gently.

Michael's eyes closed and his head fell back. "Ah, Clemmie."

Underneath her hand, she could feel the fierce pounding of his heart. For her, nothing existed except the moment and the brief stolen pleasure of being almost naked, almost in his arms.

Suddenly Michael's eyes were open, and he was studying her with such undisguised passion that even she couldn't mistake his intent. His hands ran down the length of her arms, raising goose bumps. Catching her hands, he lifted them to his lips, first one and then the other, planting one hot, moist kiss in each palm. When he released her hands, he caught her at the waist and began circling his thumbs on the silk across her abdomen.

She felt branded. And scared. And joyful. And absolutely determined not to say anything to spoil the moment.

Michael slid his hands down over her silk-clad thighs. The fire in his eyes glowed brighter as one hand moved around the front of her slip and lightly traced every curve and hollow of her body.

"You were designed for love, my darling."

She willed herself not to tremble under his touch.

"Do you know what you do to me, Clemmie?"

"Yes ... No."

His chuckle was rueful. "It's just as well."

He leaned so close she could feel his warm breath against her cheek. Almost, she could feel his lips against hers.

Suddenly he released her. His expression was grim as he turned to her closet and jerked her robe off the hanger. He wrapped it around her, not bothering with sleeves, and held it tightly closed under her chin.

"Never let a strange man into your bedroom, Clemmie."

Taking a deep breath, she fought the cry of anguish that rose in her throat.

"You're not a stranger, Michael. You're my friend."

"Woman are never my friends, Clemmie... And don't you forget that." He walked to the window and stood with his back to her.

There was defiance in his stance, and defeat, too. Clemmie saw it all. She felt an intense urge to put her arms around him and comfort him, murmur sweet soothing words in his ear. But she instinctively knew that he would reject such a gesture. Michael Forrest exuded a raw power and sexual magnetism that made her weak and yet he aroused protective instincts that made her feel strong. She wanted to love him and comfort him and laugh with him and share secret jokes with him. She wanted to touch him, to hold him, to be consumed by him. But most of all, at this moment, she wanted to understand him.

She put her arms into the sleeves and belted her robe. "You look tired, Michael."

"It's the price of debauchery." He turned around and leaned against the windowsill. "I partied the night away, then rented a motel room in Tupelo. I slept in my clothes."

"Why?"

"That's the kind of man I am—lawless and unreliable."

"Oh, Michael."

For a moment he gazed at her, his face vulnerable. Then he assumed his careless pose. She could almost see the mask drop over his face.

"You have something I want, Clemmie." Walking past her, he reached into the closet and pulled out his coat. "This."

"I was going to return it—after church."

He lifted her chin with one finger, but it was a careless touch, calculated and unfeeling.

"I know that, because that's the kind of woman you are, reliable and trustworthy."

"You make me sound like a good used car."

"You're more like a golden Chariot that's going to carry some man straight to heaven." Leaning down, he brushed his lips lightly across her cheek. "Goodbye, Clemmie."

"Goodbye?"

"Yes. I'm leaving. My bags are in the car and a check for a week's rent is on the dresser in my room."

"I thought you were staying . . . I can't possibly accept a week's rent for two days."

"You have no choice." Releasing her, he strode quickly to the door. In the doorway, he turned. "Keep singing those sweet songs, Clemmie."

Then he disappeared down the hallway.

Clemmie groped her way blindly to her bed and sank onto the mattress. Her golden man was gone. In the distance she heard the engine of his rental car roar to life. She put her hands over her ears to block out the sound. Michael Forrest was on his way back to Hollywood, and she was left with her canned pickles and her eccentric boarders and her leaky faucets and her foolish dreams.

With the music of Verdi crashing around her, she rose from the bed and began to dress. She'd be late for church, but once in a lifetime didn't matter. After all, it wasn't every day a man like Michael Forrest walked out of her life.

She pulled the red sweater over her head, then reached for her brush. Her hand stopped in mid-air. He was coming back. Hadn't he said he was making a movie in Peppertown? He'd be back with his crew, and when he returned things would be different.

She'd say, "I'm so glad you came back," and he'd say . . . She dragged the brush through her hair, planning just how it would be when Michael returned.

She was still making plans when she slid into the back pew of the church. Picking up her hymnbook, she joined the congregation in song—"Love Lifted Me."

Chapter Six

Michael surveyed the crowd.

Two hundred people were milling around the brightly lit ballroom in his house, drinking too much, laughing too loud, and telling too many lies. That's the way Hollywood parties were, he reflected, glitzy and boisterous and shallow.

As the waiter passed by, he took another glass of Baron Philippe de Rothschild's Opus One and lifted it to his lips. The red wine was smooth and rich, and it did absolutely nothing to make him forget the woman he'd left in Peppertown three days earlier.

"Michael! Darling!" A glamorous blonde took his arm and pouted at him. "Where have you been keeping yourself?"

He made no attempt to be charming. Giving her a bored smile, he asked, "Denise, isn't it?"

"Oh, Michael! You're such a tease. I'm Darlene. Remember Acapulco?"

"Should I?"

"You said you'd never forget . . . and a year later you hardly remember my name." She pouted again. "Shame on you. You'll have to do something wonderful to make it up to me."

His gaze roamed over her. She was soft and voluptuous, her blue sequined gown clinging in exactly the right spots and baring just enough skin to entice. Vaguely the memories came back. They'd been on location; she'd had a bit part in his picture.

"You love dancing on the beach. Right?"

"Right! How clever of you, darling." She took his arm. "And what else do I love?"

He merely arched his eyebrows, preferring to let her take the lead.

"The moonlight, Michael. Remember how I love to feel the moon on my skin?"

He remembered. She'd provided some nice after-hours entertainment. Maybe tonight she could provide forgetfulness.

"Dance, Darlene? For old times' sake?"

"As long as you hold me close. I like to cuddle the man I'm dancing with."

He remembered now that that's what he'd liked about Darlene: she got right to the point. And she expected nothing from him except a good time.

He gave his empty glass to a passing waiter, led her onto the dance floor, and pulled her close. His conscience pricked him. Before his trip to Peppertown, he'd have sworn he didn't even have a conscience. And now he was feeling like a cur for using one woman to forget another.

Darlene's shoulders were bare above the sequined gown. He slid his hands across that expanse of soft white flesh, hoping to feel excitement, desire, anything except the slow dull pain that weighted him down. Clemmie. Her image came to him as bright and shining as a hummingbird on the wing. He remembered the look of her, the feel of her. Her shoulders had been slim and firm and lightly tanned. And they had turned his heart inside out.

He missed a step.

"What's the matter, darling?"

"Sorry. Lack of concentration." He eased Darlene back so he could get through the dance without her too soft, too voluptuous body pressed close to him. Suddenly he discovered that he didn't want to forget with Darlene . . . or with any other woman.

She gave him a puzzled look, but continued the dance. Michael thought it would never end. When it did, he led her toward the buffet table, picked up two glasses of wine and handed one to her.

"For me?" Her smile was inviting. "I always love gifts."

"Take the drink, Darlene, but don't accept any more cheap imitations of love."

She started to laugh; then seeing the look on his face, she stopped. "You're joking, of course."

"No. Even rakes sometimes have a conscience." Leaning over, he gave her a friendly kiss on the cheek. "Thanks for the dance, Darlene. Enjoy the rest of the party."

He walked away, the music pulsing around him. The orchestra he'd hired was playing some awful modern number that didn't even have a tune. As he slipped through the crowded room, people clapped him on the shoulder and told him what a great party he was having. All he could do was nod and smile and keep on walking, for his mind was in another time, another place. Even though he was in the middle of what the gossip columns were sure to call one of the most glamorous events of the season, he was seeing a dark-haired woman in a white cotton gown. Clemmie.

He slipped through the French doors and stepped out into his courtyard. A soft California breeze whispered around him, sighing her name. Clemmie. His hand tightened on the stem of his glass of wine; then with a muttered curse, he flung the glass against a stone wall. The red wine stained the white wall, and the Baccarat crystal splintered onto the brick pavement with a careless tinkle.

Michael didn't even bother to inspect the damage. Instead, he left his party and went to his basement gymnasium. Pulling off his tuxedo jacket, he attacked his punching bag. He fought it viciously, with elbows and fists and feet. Sweat lathered his body. He stripped off his shirt and continued his attack.

As long as there was plenty to drink, his guests would never miss him. He'd deliberately planned a guest list of casual acquaintances, almost strangers, and celebrity hangers on. His presence wasn't needed. His butler would show them out.

He continued fighting the punching bag, working with such single-minded determination he didn't have time to think about his reasons for avoiding his real friends, for surrounding himself with people he barely knew, for giving the kind of party he hated.

Two hours later he went back upstairs. All his guests were gone and the orchestra members were packing their instruments away. He thanked them for a good job and went up the curving staircase to his bedroom.

He didn't bother to turn on the lights. Crossing to a chair by the window, he sat in the dark, thinking. He'd run away from Clemmie, and it hadn't worked. She was as much a part of his thoughts as if she were sitting across the room from him. What in the hell was the matter with him? Why hadn't he taken her to bed the way he would any other desirable woman? And what in the devil was he going to do about her when he went back to Peppertown to film his movie?

There would be no way to avoid her. Peppertown was too small. Groaning, he closed his eyes, but her image was stamped on his eyelids.

"Damn!" He jumped out of his chair and strode across his room. Jerking off his pants, he headed for the shower.

He turned the cold water on full force. It raised goose bumps...and it cleared his head. There was only one way he could get that innocent vamp out of his system, and that was take her to bed and prove to himself that she was just an ordinary woman. She wanted him: she'd said as much. Nothing would stand in his way this time—not conscience, not nobility, not scruples.

After all, he was a careless rake.

A week after his party, Michael Forrest was back in Peppertown. This time he had with him his seventy-five member movie company.

A pasture five miles from Clemmie's boarding house had been transformed. Trailers for the cast and crew had been set up underneath a sheltering of pine trees. A large tent with a gaily striped top served as a temporary dining room. Flatbed trucks and cranes and cameras were being unloaded.

Michael and his publicist, Jay Wilkins, stood outside his trailer, just finishing a press conference with three local newspapers and the area television station.

"Is it true, Mr. Forrest, that after your initial visit, you came back to Peppertown because you consider this location to be the most suitable for your horror movie?" The television reporter, Larry Hammond, stuck his microphone into Michael's face.

"That is partially true. Peppertown has a small-town ambience that is perfect for my movie." He looked straight into the camera and gave a wicked grin. "But there is another reason I came back to Peppertown."

"And what is that reason, Mr. Forrest?"

"A woman."

The reporter looked flustered, but he recovered quickly. "Well, now, Mr. Forrest, our audience loves a human interest story. Are you going to tell us who this woman is?"

"Yes. The woman is Clementine Brady."

"You mean Clementine Brady, the owner of Brady's Boarding House?" The resourceful reporter had done his background research. He knew everything about the town that had been selected as a movie site, and he knew much about its citizens. "And what are your plans for Miss Brady?"

"Romance, Mr. Hammond. I plan to give Miss Brady the romance of the century."

The excited reporter turned and faced the camera. "You heard it right here on WPEP. Famous Hollywood producer, Michael Forrest, has vowed to romance local beauty, Miss Clementine Brady. And he's promised it will be the romance of the century! This is Larry Hammond on the set of *Moonlight Madness* wishing you *good night*."

* * *

Clementine Brady nearly fell off the sofa.

She was sitting in her quiet, orderly parlor with Miss Josephine and Harvey when she heard Michael announce her name on the ten o'clock news.

"Good grief!" She put her hands on her hot cheeks.

"My Lord." Harvey propped his bony elbows on his knees and leaned forward. "That man has his gall."

Clemmie plucked at Harvey's sleeve. "Shh. I want to hear this." Her heart pumped so hard when he announced his intentions that she was sure Harvey would hear.

"What'd he say?" yelled Miss Josephine.

"He said he was going to romance her," Harvey shouted.

"Finance?"

"Romance!"

"St Peter's britches," Clemmie said. "Now the whole town knows."

Harvey jumped up off the sofa and cocked his fists. "I'll take care of that rascal. Just tell me what you want me to do, Clemmie."

She sat on the sofa, too stunned to think. Then she was suddenly filled with such energy and enthusiasm that she felt as if she could slip-cover Texas and still have enough strength left over to sew a ruffle around Arkansas. She smiled up at Harvey.

"What I want you to do, Harvey, is sit back and watch the fun."

"The fun?"

"Yes. If Michael Forrest thinks I'm going to be intimidated by his public announcement, he's sadly mistaken. I'm going to give him a dose of his own medicine."

The next morning the newspaper headline was "Romance of the Century."

Standing in her front hallway, Clemmie read the article with great interest. She hadn't had her name in the newspaper since she'd been valedictorian of her high school graduating class. To have her name linked with a Hollywood producer right on the front page of the paper for all of Peppertown to see was exciting and invigorating and slightly naughty. For the first time in thirty years she felt like a woman of mystery, a glamorous, decadent woman, who probably had shady secrets in her past.

Laughing, she threw the newspaper onto the hall table and went into her bedroom to dress. She rejected everything that looked the least bit sensible and settled on a pair of black wool slacks and her red turtleneck sweater. She even delved into the jewelry box she'd ignored for years and came up with a pair of red rhinestone earrings. Heaven only knew how long she'd had them or why she'd bought them in the first place.

Today she was going to shed her reliable and trustworthy image. Today she was going to call Michael Forrest's bluff.

She detoured by the small room that served as her office long enough to call her minister.

"Reverend Donwitty, this is Clemmie. Do you think you can get Miss Cates to come in today to answer the phone?"

She heard him clear his throat. He always did that when he was talking on the telephone. "Of course I can, child. You're not sick, are you?"

"No. But there is an important matter I need to take care of. If Miss Cates will handle the phone, I'll type the church bulletin at home."

"Don't worry about that, Clemmie. I'm sure Miss Cates can do that, too."

Clemmie thanked him. She left the house, then climbed into her car and set out to locate the man who had promised her the romance of the century.

He wasn't hard to find. Nearly everyone in Peppertown had watched the arrival of the movie company, and most of them knew its location.

When Clemmie arrived at the converted pasture, she parked under a large oak tree and went to find Michael.

He was sitting in a chair conveniently labeled Producer. Better yet, he was surrounded by important-looking people.

Her audience wouldn't be as big as Michael's had been last night when he'd made his startling announcement on television, but she'd have the advantage of seeing their faces. She pressed her hands together for courage; then she lifted her chin and walked into the lion's den.

"Hello, Michael."

The look of surprise on his face pleased her. He'd probably thought she'd be cowering in her boarding house, scared out of her wits about what he planned to do.

"Clemmie." Smiling, he rose to take her hand. "You look . . . stunning."

She noticed the small hesitation as he took in her red sweater and the rhinestone earrings. Let him call her reliable now. Clearly she was at an advantage, but she knew she wouldn't have it for long. Michael Forrest was not a man easily caught off balance. She pressed forward while she still could.

"I saw you on television, Michael."

Grinning, he lifted one eyebrow. It was the wicked and knowing smile that spurred her on.

"I accept your proposal."

His smile wavered, then vanished. "What?"

"Your proposal of marriage," she said, smiling sweetly. "I accept."

Michael retreated into a stunned silence.

The men, who had been watching their exchange with great interest, exploded into laughter.

Michael's publicist punched him on the shoulder. "Say, old man, this must be Clementine Brady."

"Quite a spunky gal, Mike." A red-haired giant of a man held his hand out to Clemmie. "Richard Love, Miss Brady. And I can't tell you how delighted I am to meet you. Anyone who can get one up on Michael Forrest has my undying devotion and respect."

Clemmie took his hand. She hadn't had this much fun since she'd won a blue ribbon in the cherry pie contest at the fair.

"You accept my proposal, do you?" Michael's roar took some of the edge off her euphoria. "Well, darling, don't just stand there. Let's seal the bargain."

Now it was her turn to be nonplussed.

"Seal the bargain?"

"Naturally." Without so much as even glancing at their audience, he pulled her into his arms. "You haven't forgotten how to kiss, have you?"

"In front of them?"

"Of course. Ours is going to be a very public romance."

Before she had time to reflect that her plan had backfired, Michael's lips were on hers. His kiss was hungry and very thorough—so thorough that if he hadn't kept his arm around her waist, her knees would have buckled.

When it was over, they were both somewhat breathless.

"Bravo, Michael, Clemmie. This is going to be quite a show." The man who spoke leaned over and took Clemmie's hand. "Jay Wilkins. And you've livened up this set more than you can imagine. Michael was a regular lion before you showed up."

Although she was still shaking inside from Michael's kiss, she managed to smile. "I'm glad I could help."

Rick Love hooted with laughter. "Help! Sweetheart, you've declawed that old lion and turned him into a regular tabby cat. What I want you to do is stick around this set so everybody can have the pleasure of seeing how you wrap Michael Forrest around your little finger."

"Watch you step, Richard. I'm still the boss around here. I can always get DePriest to come in and direct."

There was no doubt in anybody's mind that Michael was only teasing. The grin on his face was a dead giveaway.

Richard and Jay exchanged significant glances, then made their excuses and faded into the scenery.

"You can let go now," Clemmie said. "Our audience has vanished."

"Let go? I don't intend to let you go, Clemmie. Not while I'm in Peppertown." Michael's hold on her tightened. "Surely you didn't misunderstand me. I thought I made my intentions perfectly clear last night on television."

"I understand that you intend to play a game with me, Michael. You told me once that women are merely your playthings."

"And are you playing games with me, Clemmie? Or was that kiss real?"

She knew that if she told the truth, she'd be out of the game before it even started. If she wanted to grab this brief pleasure while she could, she'd have to lie. Although she wasn't very good at it, she'd give it a try.

"Why, Michael. I'm surprised at you. Don't you know that I could never take any man seriously? I have obligations to my brothers and to my boarders. I'm committed to my life in Peppertown." She placed her palm against his cheek. "I have no intention of taking our kisses seriously."

"In that case, we might as well do it again."

Clemmie had time to take a deep breath before Michael's mouth covered hers again.

Chapter Seven

Michael fought for control.

With Clemmie in his arms once more, he had a hard time playing his dangerous game. She smelled like honeysuckle and cinnamon and tasted of mint. The combination of tartness and sweetness almost drove him mad. Unconsciously he crushed her so close the beating of their hearts blended together in a wild, erratic rhythm.

Her lips were soft and yielding and so sensuous he almost forgot his purpose: to prove to himself that she was just another woman in his life, one he could bed and leave at his leisure.

He renewed his assault, delving deep into the honeyed sweetness of her mouth. She twisted her hands into his hair and pulled him closer. *Aw, Clemmie,* he thought. *Don't trust me so*.

"Michael." Half dazed, he lifted his head to look at his director. Richard had a knowing grin on his face. "We're ready for the first monster sequence. You *did* say you wanted to supervise.''

"Yeah. Be right with you." He cupped Clemmie's flushed face. "Do you want to stay and watch this?"

"I'd love to, if you're sure it's all right."

"It's more than all right: it's what I want." Taking her hand, he led her toward a group of people standing on the fringes of a set that resembled the inside of a science laboratory. Michael patted her cheek. "Stay right here, Clemmie, and remember where we were. After this is over, we'll take up where we left off."

She caught her lower lip between her teeth and nodded. She couldn't trust herself to speak. She was afraid of saying something foolish such as "Michael, you make me believe that I'm more than your plaything."

The sequence Michael's company was shooting involved the creation of a monster in the laboratory. Clemmie watched with fascination as the actors did the scene over and over again. They never seemed to tire.

Michael was also tireless. She'd never seen a man who generated so much enthusiasm and energy—and so much respect. When he spoke, everybody on the set listened. She was proud of him. It gave her a warm feeling to watch him work.

The director yelled "Cut," and Michael came toward her, smiling.

"Are you ready for lunch, Clemmie?"

"Lunch? It can't be that late, can it?"

"Then you weren't bored."

"How could I possibly be bored?" She caught his hand and squeezed. "Michael, you create magic. I'm fascinated."

And she was, too. Michael could tell by the glow on her face and the sincerity in her voice. He couldn't remember the last time he'd fascinated a woman. It felt good.

"It's all in a day's work, Clemmie."

They had lunch with the rest of the company underneath the striped tent. There was a great deal of good-natured teasing and jostling as the actors and the crew vied for places in the line. The aroma of corned beef and cabbage filled the air.

"Sometimes we cater our food," Michael explained to Clemmie, "but this time we brought our own cooks. They wanted to come to Mississippi and see if they could pick up some first-hand knowledge of Southern cooking."

"I'd be happy for them to visit me at the boarding house."

"I knew you would."

"How did you know?"

"I discovered two things about you: you're a great cook and you're generous enough to share your cooking secrets."

She laughed. "What I do is no secret. I'm merely using the skills my grandmother taught me."

They sat down at a table that faced the sunlit, color-splashed woods. Michael watched her closely as she bit into her corned beef.

She colored under his steady gaze. Finally she put down her food. "What is it, Michael?"

"You are very tempting." He reached for her hand and lifted it to his lips. "And you make me very hungry."

She could hear the sound of her blood pounding in her ears. "Then eat your sandwich."

"Not for food, my love. Hungry for you."

She wished she could believe him. She wanted so much for his romantic words to be real. But she knew he was only playing a game. For that matter, so was she. She was playing his game, and then, when he left Peppertown for good, no one would be hurt.

"Are you planning to seduce me in front of an audience?" She nodded toward all the people underneath the tent.

"Would you like that?"

"I've always imagined a more private seduction."

"You've imagined us together?" A light sprang to life in the center of his eyes.

"Well, yes." Without taking her eyes off his, she flicked her tongue over the bottom lip. "I'm afraid I'm very brazen."

He threw back his head and roared with laughter. "Clemmie, you are the least brazen woman I know. Come, love, tell me what you imagined."

How could she deny him anything when he looked at her like that—with tenderness and good humor and something almost like love? "Us together in a brass bed." The look on his face made her feel hot all over. She rushed on to cover her embarrassment. "The first day you came—when I showed you the upstairs room and saw you in the sunlight beside my brass bed, I pictured you there. Us there . . . together."

"And?"

"That's all. I didn't think about . . ."

"What?"

"Well, you know . . . what we were doing there."

"I did." His voice was as rich as velvet and as silky as seduction. He lifted her hand to his lips once more. "And I have. Many times."

"You thought about me?"

Endlessly, he wanted to say. "Sometimes," he said. "I thought about peeling away all those layers of white cotton you wear until I have you naked in my arms. I imagined what it would be like to make love with an innocent woman. I don't think I've ever had an innocent woman, Clemmie."

She fought to keep her disappointment from showing. Of course, Michael hadn't thought about her specifically. She was merely a new plaything for him, someone to provide a little fun while he was in Peppertown. Briefly she questioned why she would settle for that. But she didn't wonder for long. Her social life was as flat and dull as yesterday's cold pancakes. Michael Forrest was her big chance to change that, even if the change would be only temporary. She'd take what she could get.

"The bedroom is still empty, Michael."

Something shattered inside him. He didn't want Clemmie to be easy. "Don't rush things, my darling. Half the fun of the game is the chase."

"Oh, yes. The statement you made on television. You have a reputation to uphold."

He admired her control. For an innocent woman, she handled herself with great aplomb in this situation.

"Precisely. Our public is expecting the romance of the century. And as much as I want to share your bed, my dear, I'll just have to wait. I never disappoint the public." Standing, he helped her up. "Will you stay for the afternoon's shooting?"

She was tempted. Here on the movie set with this golden man she could pretend that the romance between them was real and the promises he'd made meant forever. But reality was waiting for her back at Brady's Boarding House.

"I'd love to, Michael, but I have some errands to run, and I want to write letters to my brothers."

She turned to leave, but he pulled her into his arms. "What's a romance, without a goodbye kiss?" He spread his palm over her right cheek, then slowly moved his hand around the back of her head so her hair could sift through his outspread fingers.

He held her for a small eternity, oblivious of the comments from the people who drifted by. And when he let her go, he was as flushed as she.

"Until we meet again, Clementine."

"Bye, Michael."

She didn't know it was possible to float through space, but that's what she did, positively floated toward her car. As she slid into the front seat and gripped the steering wheel, she decided that love must give one wings. She turned her key and the roar of the ignition brought a sense of reality. *Love?* What was she thinking about? She couldn't possibly fall in love with a man from Hollywood, even if that man was Michael Forrest.

She looked back one last time before she left the movie set. Michael was standing with a group of actors, and the sun was shining on his hair. It was one more memory she would store in her heart and treasure forever.

Clemmie was already dressed for bed that evening when she heard the commotion beneath her window.

Her bare feet made soft slapping sounds as she hurried across the room. What she saw took her breath away.

"Michael?" she called out the window.

"Yes. It's me." The moonlight slashed across his face, accenting his devilish grin.

"Is that a horse?"

Laughing, he stilled the prancing animal. "It's not canned pickles."

He urged the magnificent white stallion closer to her window. Dressed in black pants, shiny black boots and a big-sleeved, open-necked white shirt that exposed his chest, he looked like a buccaneer.

Clemmie had never seen such a sight except on the movie screen. She was enchanted.

"What in the world are you doing at my window at this hour?"

"That's how Romeo courted Juliet."

"We're not Romeo and Juliet."

"No. You're Sleeping Beauty and I'm Prince Charming." Sitting atop the horse, he gave her a gallant bow. "At your service."

She loved this playful mood of his. Leaning her elbows on her windowsill, she smiled at him.

"You're getting your fairy tales confused."

"Tonight, love, we're going to create our own fairy tale."

"But, Michael, it's late and I'm dressed in my gown."

"A gown I'd love to rip apart with my bare hands." His eyes burned over her, then he gave a dramatic sigh. "Alas, we have a reputation to uphold." He reached into a saddlebag, pulled out a package and handed it through the window. "Here, put this on. We're going riding."

She stared at the white box. "What in the world..."

"Just a little something I snitched from wardrobe."

She opened the box and lifted out a green velvet dress with a tight bodice, scooped neck and billowing skirt. It was an enchanting costume. Holding it across her chest, she beamed. "How did you know my size?"

"I've studied you, Clemmie." He paused, watching her. "God, Clemmie, if you knew what those blushes do to me, you wouldn't keep blushing like that. Get dressed before I change my mind and take you up those stairs to that brass bed.''

"You won't look?"

He fought a battle with himself to keep from pulling her through the window, throwing her across the saddle and disappearing with her forever.

"I won't look. I promise." He flicked the reins and the white horse trotted toward the gazebo.

Clemmie's hands shook as she slipped out of her gown and fastened the tiny hooks on the green velvet bodice. The dress was a perfect fit. She never doubted for a second that Michael had told the truth about studying her body. The thought made her feel warm inside.

Taking a deep breath, she went outside to join him.

He watched her cross the yard. In the green velvet dress with the moonlight shining on her skin, she looked like every man's dream come true. She could be so easy to love. *Careful,* he told himself. *Don't get caught up in your own game.*

When she was close enough, he slid off his horse and circled her waist.

"Are you ready?"

"For what, Michael?"

"Romance, Clemmie."

He swung her onto the horse and mounted behind her. They galloped through Peppertown, causing heads to turn as they passed the ordinary travelers consigned to their functional Fords and serviceable Chevrolets. The wind caught Michael's exultant laughter and carried it to the ears of a few late-night customers standing outside Woody's Cafe.

Leaning close to Clemmie's ear, he said, "By morning, the whole town will be telling this story."

"I hope so."

"You do?"

"Oh, yes. This is the most extraordinary thing that has happened in Peppertown in a long time. I'm glad to be a part of it."

Michael wondered why he was being so richly rewarded for such a selfish act. Men who set out to lure innocent women to their beds shouldn't be made to feel like kings. And yet, he did. With Clemmie's back pressing against his chest and her silky hair blowing against his cheek, he felt as if he had captured a priceless treasure and was on his way to save the world. If this foolishness persisted, he was likely to lose track of his purpose. As he turned the stallion toward the movie encampment, he vowed that he wouldn't be caught in his own trap. He'd remember that this was not love but merely a game.

He brought the horse to a halt underneath a large pine tree.

"Here we are, my love."

Clemmie turned to look at him. "We're back at your movie set, aren't we?"

"Yes." He brushed his hand across her cheek, wanting to absorb its softness into his soul. "I have a surprise for you. Close your eyes."

"I love surprises."

Clemmie felt like a child at Christmas as Michael led her across the pasture. Night breezes stirred her hair, and she could hear the mournful hooting of owls deep in the woods beyond the camp.

"We're almost there, Clemmie. Keep your eyes closed." Letting go of her hand, he caught her shoulders and guided her through the opening of a tent. She felt the canvas brush against her cheek and heard the metallic clang as Michael's boot scraped against a tent pole. "You can open your eyes now."

The dining tent had been transformed. White silk hangings tied back with heavy gold tassels were draped around the canvas walls. A table for two was set with white linen cloth, glowing candles in a crystal candelabra, and golden mums in a silver bowl. Michael walked toward a table and punched the tape player button. The music of Verdi's *La Traviata* filled the tent.

"Oh, Michael, this is magic. How did you ever do it?"

"With a little help from props and wardrobe, I'm a master at creating magic." He took her hand and smiled down at her. "Do you like it, Clemmie?"

"I love it."

Michael bent over her hand with a deep, formal bow. "May I have this dance, Sleeping Beauty?"

"Certainly, Prince Charming."

They danced cheek to cheek and heart to heart in the temporary splendor of the canvas tent.

"You even got my favorite opera. How did you know, Michael?"

"I guessed. Remember that day in your bedroom? You were playing Verdi when I came to get my coat."

"I'll never forget that day."

"Nor will I."

He pulled her closer as they moved together in perfect rhythm. Michael thought there had never been a woman who fit into his arms so well, and Clemmie thought there had never been a man who could make her feel as if she had wings.

They danced for almost an hour, whirling around the tent, Clemmie's velvet skirt brushing against Michael's thigh and her hair softly caressing his cheek.

When the music had ended, Michael held her at arm's length. "We dance well together, Clemmie."

"Yes, we do."

They were too good together, and that was his problem. He sought to put their relationship into proper perspective by a careless remark.

"I wonder if we will be that good together in bed?"

She tried to stifle her sharp intake of breath. But she could tell by the tight look on Michael's face that he heard.

"I don't know, Michael. I've never—"

Interrupting, he put a finger on her lips. "Shh. Don't talk. Just let me hold you."

Attacks of conscience were new to Michael, but he was immediately contrite for putting a damper on Clemmie's evening. She'd been having a wonderful time. He had, too. Maybe that's why he'd brought up the subject of seduction: to remind both of them that tonight was merely a charade, that it had nothing to do with love and romance and living happily ever after. He knew firsthand that there was no such thing as happily ever after.

He held her close for a moment, rubbing his hands across her back, trying to massage away the tension that had been caused by his remark. She held herself stiff in his arms, and he knew that she was fighting for control. He sensed that she was struggling to play a role totally unfamiliar to her, that of casual flirt.

Catching the back of her head, he pressed her down onto his shoulder.

"I'm sorry I said that, Clemmie."

"It's all right, Michael. I know this is only pretend." She pasted a brave, false smile on her face and lifted her head to look at him. "You've made your intentions perfectly clear. And I'm an adult. I'm doing this with my eyes wide open.''

He cupped her face. ''You're sweet, Clemmie, and far too generous.''

''Why, Michael, you're the one who is generous.'' She stepped out of his arms and lifted the sides of the velvet skirt. ''Just look at this dress. What other woman in Peppertown has ever worn a dress that Scarlett O'Hara might have worn? And this tent.'' She swung her arm around to encompass the white draperies, the crystal and flowers, the music of Verdi. ''It's like being in the middle of a dream.'' She moved close and put her right hand on his cheek. ''You don't give yourself enough credit. You're a warm and generous and caring man. The only thing I don't understand is why you're doing all this for me instead of some glamorous Hollywood woman more suited to a man like you.''

Clemmie's gentle touch and compassionate face thawed some frozen corner of his soul. For the first time in his life he felt a need to tell someone why he'd shunned permanent relationships with women.

''You have no idea what those glamorous women are like, do you?''

''I imagine they're sophisticated and successful. But they are probably somewhat pressured and a little bit insecure.''

He took her hand and led her to the table. ''I never thought of them in that way, Clemmie. It never occurred to me that Hubbard might have been feeling pressured and insecure.''

''Hubbard Gladstone?''

The minute he'd let her name slip, Michael was sorry. His life-style hinged on keeping his thoughts to himself. How could he tell this sweet, enticing woman sitting across the table from him that the scandal sheets had told only part of the story? That he'd actually wanted Hubbard's child to be his? That although he hadn't actually loved her, he would have married her to give that child a name?

Leaning his chair back on two legs, he gave Clemmie a cocky smile. "That's right. The woman who sued me for paternity."

"Michael, don't try so hard to shock me. I understand that people are only human."

The legs of the chair hit the ground with a bang. "Dammit, Clemmie, if you keep this up, I'll have to have you bronzed and put on a pedestal. No woman should be as sweet and understanding and damned *kind* as you are."

She folded her hands on her lap and tried not to look as if she'd just won the *Reader's Digest* Sweepstakes. "I don't think I could have any fun up there on a pedestal. I prefer to have both feet on the ground."

He tipped his head back and roared with laughter. "Don't worry, you do. Everybody is still talking about the way you walked boldly in here this morning and put me in my place."

"Did I embarrass you, Michael?"

"No, you delighted me. And surprised me, too. I can't remember when I've had so much fun. It's not every day a man in my position gets his comeuppance, especially from a woman."

"You were doing fine until you got to the part about *especially from a woman*." She was feeling much more relaxed now that the matter of the bed was closed. She had missed her little sparring matches with Michael after he'd gone back to Hollywood. She'd missed having him around the house too. He was the kind of man who made a house seem *full*. His booming laughter, his stunning good looks, his wit, his vitality—all had a way of putting life into a house. Oh, she'd miss him when he was gone, she thought. It would be like chopping off a part of herself and sending it away.

She leaned forward in her chair and smiled at him. "But I'll forgive you for that sexist remark because you're such a nice guy."

If it was possible for a person to beam, Michael did. "Would you mind repeating that?" He held up his hand. "No, wait. Let me wake everybody up first. I want them to hear."

"Go right ahead. In fact, I'll stand on the tabletop and shout it if you like."

"You would, wouldn't you?"

"Yes, I would. Because you *are* nice, and I want everyone to know. I think I'll take out an ad in the paper."

"Or I could call a press conference and let you say it for the television audience."

They laughed together. It felt good for both of them. And right, almost like fate.

"You make me very hungry, Clemmie." He smiled at the look on her face. "For food, too. Around you I seem to have a hearty appetite for all things." Michael lifted the silver cover off a cake dish. "Fortunately I have a great chef at my beck and call." He cut a generous slice of chocolate cake and handed it to her. "A midnight snack, prepared especially for you."

"You're spoiling me."

"I want to." He leaned across the table and ran his finger across her lips. "Eat your cake, love."

While she ate, Clemmie studied Michael. The moonlight streaming through the tent flap made his snowy white pirate's shirt glow. It also softened his face, making him look approachable and very nice. He *was* nice. And generous. And wonderful. And she was dreadfully, insanely, irrevocably, irrationally head-over-heels in love with him. The revelation struck her with a force that made her catch her breath. What was she to do?

"A penny for your thoughts, Clemmie."

There was nothing to do but lie again, she thought. Confessing love to a confirmed womanizer would be a quick way to end this small adventure. "I'm wondering if all this turns into a pumpkin at midnight." She swept her hand to encompass the tent and its trimmings.

"No. This is not Cinderella. It's our own fairy tale. Remember?"

"I wish it could go on forever, but a working woman has to be practical."

"Is that a hint to take you home?"

"Would you? It's been beautiful, but I really must go."

"Your wish is my command, my darling."

He escorted her out of the tent and swept her into the saddle of the waiting white stallion. As they galloped through the night, she leaned against his chest, cherishing the last precious moments of being close to him. She'd done the right thing. Going home was the best way to protect herself, to protect him. She couldn't have spent another moment in that magical tent with the music of Verdi swooning around them without spilling her heart to him. And that would certainly have been a mistake, for Michael wasn't interested in love. He'd made that perfectly clear. If she wanted him to continue this beautiful imitation of romance, she'd have to keep her true feelings to herself.

When they reached the boarding house, Michael slid from the saddle and helped her down.

"Good night, my love."

"Good night, Michael." She hoped her voice didn't show her disappointment. She'd wanted him to kiss her, but she supposed it was just as well. Turning from him, she started into her house.

"Clemmie."

The low urgency in his voice made her whirl around. He reached her in two quick strides and circled his hands around her waist.

"If I kissed you tonight, I might never let you go."

She drew a deep breath, waiting.

His right hand came up to her face. "Such temptation."

Abruptly he released her and walked away. He swung into the saddle and spun the horse away, toward the road in front of her house. When he reached the shadows of the oak tree, he turned and looked back over his shoulder. Clemmie was still standing beside her front door. The moon spotlighted her face. It glistened. Tears? he wondered. Was Clemmie crying? Something twisted in his gut. He almost turned and galloped back across the yard to her.

"Don't be a fool." He slapped the reins and galloped off into the night, thinking that absence and distance would make him forget.

But the sight of those tears on her face haunted him all the way back to his camp.

Chapter Eight

The sound of rain on the roof woke Clemmie.

She lay in her bed, content to listen to the rain and remember last night. The velvet gown, the tent, the white stallion had been beautiful. It was the perfect setting for falling in love. She hugged her arms across her chest, remembering every look, every word, every touch Michael had given her. Was that what being in love was like? Cherishing every tiny detail?

Smiling, she rolled over and looked at the clock. Goodness gracious, she'd overslept.

She was already jerking off her gown as her feet hit the floor. She barely had her jeans on when the doorbell rang. Grabbing a blue sweatshirt, she hurried to answer the door.

"Are you Miss Clementine Brady?" The man standing on her doorstep was young, freckled, and holding the most enormous bouquet of orchids Clemmie had ever seen.

"Yes," she said.

"These are for you."

Clemmie took the flowers inside and set them on the hall table. They made even the shabby hallway look elegant. She took the card out and read, "Shall I compare thee to a summer's day? Thou art more lovely and more temperate. Michael."

One of Shakespeare's sonnets, she thought. Michael was truly a romantic.

She started toward the kitchen, then turned back and snatched the orchids off the hall table. She couldn't bear to leave them behind. She figured she'd carry them from room to room all day long, so that she could see the delicate purple blossoms and be reminded of the man she loved.

Hurrying to the kitchen, she put the orchids on the cabinet in plain view and tried to decide what sort of breakfast she could put together in five minutes. While she was standing there, Harvey stuck his head in the doorway.

"Clemmie, I heard the doorbell." Spotting the flowers, he came into the kitchen. "Nice. I don't suppose I have to ask who sent them."

"No. It was Michael."

Harvey tried to look happy for her, but only succeeded in looking like a floppy-eared puppy that had been wet down with a water hose.

"Listen, Clemmie, if you haven't already made breakfast for me, I think I'll get a bite in Fulton. We've already started rehearsals on our Christmas symphony and I need to be there early."

"Thanks, Harvey." She smiled at him. "Don't forget your umbrella. It looks like it might blow up a storm."

"I've got it. Bye, Clemmie." He waved a bony hand at her and left to get his tuba.

"Dear, sweet Harvey," she said softly. She knew that he'd seen she didn't have any breakfast prepared. She'd bet that he'd even known about her late-night date with Michael. After all, he could hardly miss a white stallion outside his window.

Clemmie quickly filled two bowls with cereal and poured two glasses of juice. With one last look at her orchids, she left the kitchen. She could hardly manage to take them and the breakfast tray at the same time.

Miss Josephine was already dressed and waiting to be helped down the stairs to breakfast. With her sprigged muslin dress, her dead corsage, and her carefully rouged face, she looked as if she might be waiting for a tea party.

She smiled when she saw Clemmie. "What a surprise, my dear. Is that breakfast?"

"Yes," Clemmie shouted. "There are only the two of us. I thought we'd eat at that table beside your window. Watching the rain will be nice."

"Well, we could eat in the stable, but why don't we eat at that table by the window? We can watch the rain."

Clemmie put the tray on the table and dragged two chairs across the floor. After they were seated, Miss Josephine regaled her with stories from her past. Clemmie knew that she was required only to listen.

"Junior took me down to Luther Whitman's for a fall barn dance. It was the end of harvest time, you see, and everybody was celebrating getting their crops in from the field. Skip Bradley had his fiddle and old man Rufus Trent had a washtub and a broom rigged up with wire. It made a lovely bass drum."

Miss Josephine paused for breath. Clemmie smiled and nodded and listened to the wind pick up speed and the rain slash against the windows. Miss Josephine wiped the juice from her mouth and continued her monologue. She described her dress in great detail. In fact, she described every dress at the barn dance.

As Clemmie listened to Miss Josephine's tales of her dear departed Junior Wade, she thought of Michael. The need to confide her love welled up inside. Why not? Miss Josephine was the perfect confidante. She would listen without hearing, and she would make no judgments and give no advice.

Miss Josephine was talking on, "Of course, Junior had kissed me before, but not like that. It was so romantic."

Clemmie filled the pause. "Michael's romantic, too. I guess that's one of the reasons I love him."

"No, dear, there weren't any doves in the barn. But there was hay. Junior pulled me behind one of the hay bales and kissed me like there was no tomorrow. That night, I thought we'd have each other forever."

"I know that I won't have forever with Michael. I'm merely an amusement for him, and even if he did fall in love with me, what in the world would we do? I can't leave Peppertown and he can't leave Hollywood. I have my brothers to take care of, and then there are my boarders. Oh, I know the schoolteachers and Harvey could find someplace else, but what would happen to you, Miss Josephine?"

"Shot right in the stomach. That's what happened." Clemmie jumped when Miss Josephine snapped her fingers. She'd been so caught up in her own confessions, she'd hardly been paying attention to what the old lady said. "Just like that," Josephine continued. "I'll never forget that day they came and told me he'd been mistaken for a deer and shot plumb dead. Of course, my loss was Heaven's gain. Junior went up there to make some lucky angel happy. Believe you me, when I get there I'll tie a knot in her wings. Junior's still mine, and I mean to have him."

Clemmie suppressed her smile. Leaning across the table, she patted Miss Josephine's hand and murmured, "I'd love to have Michael, too. Just once, you understand. I want to know what it's like to give myself completely to the man I love."

"Of course he loves me, and you're sweet to say those nice things about my dear departed Junior. But my time's a comin'. Why, I'll walk right up to that sassy angel and say, 'You've had your turn. Now it's mine.'" Miss Josephine slapped her thigh and laughed. "Lordy, won't we have a time?"

"Yes. You will surely have a time."

"Somebody's committed a crime?" Miss Josephine's hands fluttered up to her face like two withered butterflies. "Why, child, why didn't you say something sooner? Why we could all be murdered in our sleep. I'm anxious to see Junior again, but not that anxious. Mercy me!"

Clemmie's private confessional was over. She spent the next ten minutes dealing with Miss Josephine's latest fantasy, then picked up the breakfast dishes and carried them down the stairs.

Thunder rumbled and lightning flashed. The old boarding house trembled under nature's onslaught, its shutters clattering and its windows rattling. Clemmie was happy to see the rain, but she worried about her house. Taking her flashlight she went into the attic to see if her roof had sprung any new leaks. Much to her relief, there were no telltale puddles on the hardwood floor, and the beam of the light picked up no damp patches on the ceiling.

She stood in the middle of the crowded attic, giving thanks for small blessings. In the corner her sewing machine beckoned to her. While she was up there, she might as well finish sewing that shirt she'd started two weeks ago for Daniel. She'd planned to return the velvet dress to Michael and thank him for the orchids, but she'd wait until the rain slackened. She didn't like driving in a downpour. And besides, surely the company would not be filming in this weather. The chances were small that they would need the green velvet dress.

The rain came down without mercy.

By five o'clock that afternoon, Clemmie had decided she'd better go ahead and return the dress. The weatherman had predicted rain for the next two days. Putting on her boots and raincoat and tucking the velvet dress and its box carefully into a plastic garment bag, she headed for her car.

She knew it was foolish to go out in such a rain, but what if Michael needed that velvet dress for one of his scenes? She certainly didn't want to be responsible for holding up a motion picture simply because she didn't like driving in the rain. No sir, she thought as she opened her umbrella and stepped outside. It would be dark soon. She'd best go while she still had some daylight left.

A gust of high wind got under the hem of her raincoat and whipped it up around her legs. Fighting to keep the rain-slicked garment bag from slipping out of her hand, she jerked at the garage door. For once it cooperated.

In a matter of minutes Clemmie was easing her car out of her driveway and creeping through Peppertown. Her hands gripped the steering wheel and she leaned forward, squinting so she wouldn't miss the turnoff.

She didn't know what she'd expected when she got to the movie encampment. Certainly not the bedlam she saw. With her motor still running and her wipers going, she peered through the windshield. It looked as if the company was moving full speed ahead. Bright neon yellow slickers shone through the gloom. They were everywhere—perched atop the crane, huddled behind the cameras, clumped in the canvas director's chair. She thought she spotted Michael, but she couldn't be sure. That tall form in the yellow slicker could have been anybody.

She sat in her car a while, watching. There was no need to get out yet. She'd only add to the confusion. When she saw a break in the action, she'd sprint across the pasture and hand Michael the velvet gown. She'd say, "Thank you for letting me wear the beautiful dress. Oh, and thank you for the orchids." Then she'd leave. She wouldn't embarrass both of them by saying, "Michael, I've fallen in love with you and I don't quite know what to do about it."

Clemmie's wipers made quiet swishing noises as she watched.

The rain had been a blessing in disguise.

Michael's yellow slicker rattled as he stood up. They had needed a storm for one of their sequences, and nature had obliged. He glanced at Rick Love, sitting hunched over in his director's chair. He could tell by the look of satisfaction on his face that Rick was pleased with the day's work. The real thing was always better than special effects.

Michael was glad the day's work had gone well. Filming in this kind of weather was always tricky. And nature might not provide another storm for a retake.

Behind him, Rick yelled "Cut," and excited actors came streaming past. There was a lot of good-natured jostling and back-slapping and general high spirits as everyone released the tensions of the day.

Michael moved along in the stream of people, chatting with Lonnie Bobo, one of the lead actors, when he spotted Clemmie up ahead. She was stepping out of her car, clutching her red raincoat around her throat and holding on to a red umbrella. Michael had his hand lifted in greeting when one of the extras, a high-spirited young eighteen-year-old, head down against the rain, broke into a run and barreled into Clemmie.

She went down in a tangle of wet raincoat and spiky umbrella. Michael tore loose from the crowd and sprinted toward her.

The boy who had bowled her over was bending down, flapping his arms and apologizing. "I'm so sorry. I didn't see you. I was hurrying to my car so I could go and get a pizza."

The young jackass, Michael thought. "No harm done," he heard Clemmie say. No harm! Why she was sitting in a large puddle of water and she was wet and muddy from head to toe. She'd be damned lucky if she didn't catch pneumonia. Hell, she might even have a broken bone.

"I'll take over. She's mine." Shouldering the boy aside, he knelt beside Clemmie. He was so rattled he didn't even know what he had said.

The boy still hovered uncertainly. Clemmie smiled up at him. "I'm perfectly fine. Really. Go on and enjoy your pizza."

"You're sure?"

Michael wanted to lift him up by the seat of the britches and toss him into his car. Why didn't the young simpleton just move out of the way instead of keeping Clemmie sitting in the mud, talking? Before she could say anything else to the boy, Michael scooped her up and cradled her against his chest.

"It's all right, sweet," he murmured to her. "I'll take care of you." He stood up, kicked the ruined umbrella aside and strode off toward his trailer.

Much as Clemmie loved the idea of being carried off by the man she loved, she had a soft spot for the young man who had knocked her over. He reminded her of her brothers.

"Michael," she said, tugging on the front of his slicker, "take me back immediately."

"What?" He never even broke his stride, just kept hurrying toward his trailer as if she were a life and death case.

"I said take me back to that poor young man. He was upset."

"He damned well should be. He nearly got you killed."

She had to smile. Michael was acting worse than an overprotective grandmother. "Killed?"

"Tackling you like a linebacker. Not to mention letting you wallow around in the mud in this weather."

This time she laughed outright. "Michael, I'm perfectly fine. Just a little wet. Take me back this very minute."

By now they had attracted an audience. Rick, who had seen Clemmie go down, and Jay, who had witnessed Michael picking her up, had joined them. They didn't want to miss a bit of the action between these two.

"Like hell," Michael said, bulldozing forward.

"Then I'll go on my own." Clemmie shoved against his chest and tried to get out of his arms.

Rick and Jay hooted with laughter.

"Looks like the lady means business," Rick commented.

"Go to it, Clemmie," Jay said. "Teach the old boy some manners."

Still holding on to Clemmie, Michael whirled around and scowled at them. "Don't you two have something better to do besides gawk at me?"

"Well, we could go over to your trailer for a three-handed game of stud poker." Rick couldn't keep the knowing grin off his face.

"Or we could pick up Chinese food and bring it over," Jay said, deadpan. "Dinner for four."

"Beat it." Michael knew he'd been bested when Clemmie, Rick and Jay all burst into laughter. "Aw, hell. Where is that little pip-squeak you wanted to see?"

"Just getting into his car. If you'll put me down, I can catch him and let him know I'm all right so he won't worry."

Michael tightened his grip. "I'm not letting you out of my sight until I have you out of those wet clothes."

As he started toward the young man's blue Maverick, Rick and Jay applauded.

"I'll deal with you later," Michael yelled over his shoulder.

He thought he handled the next few minutes with fairly good grace, considering that the young idiot Clemmie was talking to kept looking at her like a love-sick puppy. Michael kept a tight hold on Clemmie the whole time she was talking. Knowing her, there was no telling what she'd do next. Hell, she might even invite the careless dolt over to her house for gingerbread.

He shouldn't complain, he thought. Standing in the pouring rain with Clemmie in his arms was a very pleasurable experience. Through the wet clothes, she was all woman. All sexy woman, he corrected, looking down at her. The rain had molded her silky raincoat against her body, outlining the proud curve of her hip, the sweet up-thrust of her breasts.

Being concerned for her welfare was slowly giving way to being aroused. When the teenager finally left, Michael stalked back to his trailer in silence.

He mounted the steps and kicked the door shut behind them. His face was fierce as he looked down at her.

"Let's get you out of those wet clothes."

The way she looked at him, with those eyes so wide and innocent and startled, socked him right in the heart. If she'd known how close he was to ripping aside her wet clothes and taking her on the carpet, she really would be frightened. Well, hell, he thought, hadn't that been his intention all along? But not yet. Not while she was shivering and wet and cold. Not with those big eyes staring at him.

"You want me to undress?"

"Yes." He put her on her feet and peeled off her wet raincoat. "I want you out of those clothes in two minutes flat."

Now that the excitement was over, she was cold, Clemmie admitted to herself. But she didn't know what Michael's intentions were. If he wanted to make love, why was he scowling? And why was he in such a hurry for her to undress? Shouldn't there be a little more romance to the whole thing?

She hugged her arms around her shoulders and shivered. Ordinarily she was content with herself exactly the way she was, but today she wished she knew what to do and say when a man said to strip off your clothes. Was she supposed to strip slowly, like Gypsy Rose Lee, one piece at a time? She could just picture it, the music blaring, the lights glinting on the stage, and Michael sitting in a front row seat, watching her. But she wasn't wearing sequins and feathers. She smiled at the idea of herself trying to look seductive swinging a soggy sweatshirt over her head.

"What's so damned funny?"

She jerked her eyes up to his. She wasn't on a stage with lights and music. She was in Michael's trailer, dripping water all over his carpet.

"Nothing. It's just that..." Her teeth began to chatter.

"Damn." Setting his mouth into a grim line, Michael tossed off his yellow slicker, then turned back to Clemmie. "If you won't get undressed, I'll do it for you. Otherwise you're going to end up with pneumonia."

"That's why you want me to get undressed?"

"Of course. What did you think?" Her bright pink cheeks told him what she had thought. "Dammit all, Clemmie. I may be a womanizer, but I'm not that bad. When I make love with a woman I do it with soft music and candlelight."

"Oh. I feel foolish."

He put a finger under her chin and tipped her face up. "You don't look foolish; you look wet and cold. And I gave you the wrong impression." Gently he took her shoulders and guided her toward his bedroom. "You can get out of your wet things in there. My robe is hanging next to the shower. Use it."

He paced the floor while she changed. The thin trailer walls weren't made to be soundproof, and he heard every sound she made. The dull thud of heavy wet jeans and sweatshirt against the floor made his heart beat faster. She'd be in her panties and bra now. He knew her shape, for he had memorized it with his hands.

A door slammed and he heard the sounds of running water. She would be in the shower now. Water spiking her eyelashes. Soap slicking down her firm, flat abdomen. He knew exactly how her soap-slick body would feel. Ripe and luscious. He groaned as he thought of his hands on her, gentling those fine curves, arousing those wet, erect nipples, plundering the sweetness of those thighs.

Only a thin wall separated them. With need and desire making his blood sing in his ears, he put his hand on the doorknob and turned. Now he'd have her. He *had* to have her.

The sound of water in the shower beckoned to him. Then he heard a new sound. Clemmie was singing.

His hand went limp on the doorknob. He couldn't do it. Now was not the time. Later, he decided as he crossed the small den and sank onto the sofa. His company would be in Peppertown a few more weeks. Why rush things?

When Clemmie came out of his shower, fresh-faced and shining, her hair wet and sexy, she was covered from chin to ankle in his green terry-cloth robe. It was then that Michael almost changed his mind. He almost pulled her onto the sofa, tore that robe apart and lost himself in her sweet flesh. A tiny shred of control saved him.

"Do you feel better now, Clemmie?"

She smiled. "Yes. Warmer, too." When she sat in the chair across the room, the robe gapped open. He caught an enticing glimpse of leg. "I didn't know I was so muddy until I saw it all wash down the shower drain."

He kept his eyes on her face, praying that her sweet, trusting smile would redeem him. "Am I the reason you came out in this storm today?"

"Yes. I was returning the green velvet dress." Even as she said the words she knew they were only part of the truth. She'd come to see Michael. Looking at him now, slouched comfortably on the awful brown sofa, she felt breathless. That dress had merely been an excuse.

"I was hoping you'd come because of my irresistible charm."

If he had meant his smile to be cocky, he wasn't fooling her. She saw his vulnerability, the brief flash of hope.

"You *are* charming, Michael, and so easy to . . . like."

"Don't be sweet to me, Clemmie."

"You've said that before. Why?"

Outside, thunder boomed and rain battered against the trailer. The weather was as wild as Michael felt. His need for Clemmie was clawing at his gut, raking along his nerve endings and setting his teeth on edge. Looking at her, curled in the tacky flowered chair that had come with the trailer, he suddenly realized his need was more than lust. He needed her approval and her understanding. He'd always thought himself immune to those feelings until this woman with the soft voice and sweet smile had taught him he was only human.

"I'm going to tell you a story," he said. "A true story." He watched her face. It didn't change. She didn't get that bored look that meant she couldn't care less. "Sweet women have never been a part of my life, Clemmie. My mother was famous, wealthy, and beautiful. She barely knew I existed."

"Oh, Michael." Clemmie pressed her hand against her throat.

"And then there was Hubbard Gladstone. She wasn't sweet, but she sure as hell was good-looking. She wasn't my first, of course, but she just lasted longer. At one point I even fancied she and I would get married."

"You loved her?"

"Love?" His eyes raked over her. "Love had nothing to do with it. I thought the child she was carrying belonged to me. That's what she wanted me to think. The real father was a penniless, out-of-work bodybuilder. She'd met him at the gym where she worked out three times a week." His laugh was short and bitter. "Some workout."

"How do you know it wasn't your child?"

"My private investigators found out about the bodybuilder. And the blood tests proved beyond a doubt that he was the father."

"You wanted a child?"

"Yes. Does that surprise you?"

"No, Michael. I think you would make a wonderful father. You have a tender side that you try to keep hidden, but I know it's there." Suddenly she pictured Michael with children, their children. There would be at least three, two boys with golden eyes like his and a daughter with his bright golden hair. The children were so real that she reached out to touch them. When her hand clutched emptiness, she was sad, almost as if her children had been snatched away from her.

"Are you crying?" Michael jumped up from the sofa and knelt on the floor beside her chair. He brushed away the telltale tear with his fingertips. His hands lingered on her face. "I didn't mean to make you sad."

"It's not you; it's the children."

"What children?"

"The ones you could have." Her smile was gentle. "I'm a dreamer, Michael. I was picturing myself in Hubbard's place—having your children." She reached out and touched his hair. "I would never have betrayed you. I would have loved you—always." Her heart tripped a beat at the way he looked at her. She flicked her tongue over her dry lips. "If I had been Hubbard..."

He stared at her in silence. When he finally spoke, it was in a hoarse whisper. "You'd be so easy to love." His hands cupped her face, then moved down the sides of her slender neck. "To wake in the morning with your face on the pillow next to mine..." His voice trailed off as his hand dipped into the top of the robe. She shivered as he dragged his fingertips lightly over her nipple. "To know that you belonged to me..." He cupped her breast, spreading his fingers wide so he could lift it up like an offering. She held her breath as he looked deep into her eyes. His free hand found her thigh between the open folds of the robe. Goose bumps rose where he touched her, but she didn't pull back. "To hear that soft voice whisper my name..." His hand caressed her leg, moving steadily upward. "To know that I was the first one to touch you..." He paused, his fingertips brushing lightly. "...here."

"Ah, Michael." Her head lolled on her limp neck. Her legs felt like rubber. "Touch me. Please, touch me."

His hand trembled on her. "Clemmie? Do you know what you're asking?"

"Yes. Oh, yes, Michael."

His hand trembled slightly, then his fingertip delved briefly into her. Ecstasy ripped through her. The finger slipped in again, then pulled out. "Don't," she whimpered. She wanted it to go on forever. "Oh, don't... stop."

She was ready for him. She wanted him. Michael knew that. As his hand sought her again, he knew he was on the edge of control. A little while longer and there would be no pulling back. His hand hovered near that sweet heat for a moment, then drew back. His conscience wouldn't let him take Clemmie simply because she was willing.

Gently he folded the robe back across her thighs. Her head snapped up. "Michael?"

"Ah, Clemmie." He bent over her and kissed the silky skin of her cleavage. "You'd be so easy to love."

"Then love me."

"I'm not the falling in love kind." He stood up and walked back to the sofa.

Clemmie saw her one chance slipping away. Now was the time. With the storm battering the trailer and nobody around to ring a cowbell or call for her attention, now was the time to be with the man she loved. She took a deep breath.

"I know that, Michael. Don't you think I do?" Slowly she stood up. "I can't make commitments, either. My brothers have three more years of college, and I'm responsible for them. I could never leave Peppertown." Love drove her; instinct guided her. Looking deep into Michael's eyes, she reached for her belt. Now that she was resolved to this drastic action, she felt an incredible calm.

"Clemmie. What are you doing?"

"Don't stop me, Michael." The knot gave way and the robe gapped open. "I know what I am doing."

Her skin glowed in the dim light of the trailer. With a shrug that was totally uncalculated, Clemmie let the robe slip from her shoulders. Her breasts were small and pointed, proudly erect and achingly sweet.

She held her head high, only the slight tremor of her lips betraying her turmoil.

"My God," he breathed. "You have no idea what you're doing." He grabbed her by the shoulders, his eyes burning over her.

"Kiss me, Michael."

"How can I refuse a lady?" His mouth came down on hers. The kiss was as fierce and wild as the storm lashing against the trailer. His tongue invaded her mouth, plundering its depths. Unconsciously she rocked against him.

"Clemmie... Oh, yes, baby...." His hands guided her hips closer, pressed her hard against him. He smiled as her eyes widened. "Now do you see what you do to me, love?"

"Yes." She tangled her hands in his hair and pulled his head down to her breasts. "I don't want to be innocent anymore, Michael. Love me."

His control snapped. How could he refuse such a tantalizing offer? he wondered. He tasted her nipples, first one, then the other. He felt the shiver run through her body. Ever so slowly, his mouth covered her breast. She moaned, arching her back so that her hips were fitted perfectly to his.

He hadn't meant to let it go this far, but with Clemmie, ready and willing in his arms, he had no more control than the storm. He drew the sweetness deep into his mouth while his hips plunged against hers. She kept his rhythm, hesitant at first, then with more certainty.

Outside the trailer the storm picked up pace, howling its fury and battering at the windows. Michael felt the same wildness building between them. His need was tinged with desperation. He wanted Clemmie more than he had ever thought it possible to want a woman and yet some part of him held back. She was offering so much and settling for so little: her virginity for a one-night stand. That didn't seem a fair exchange for him.

Groaning, he lifted his head and took her mouth once more. He had to taste her lips one last time. He had to drug himself on her sweetness before he could pull away.

He kissed her gently this time, gradually slowing the rhythm of his hips against hers, easing both of them down from the mountaintop so they wouldn't plunge over the edge.

At last he stepped back and pulled the robe onto her shoulders.

"I can't let you do this, Clemmie."

Her eyes were wide and luminous. She put a trembling hand on her throat, but said nothing.

His smile was rueful. "Scruples." He pulled the robe shut, covering the innocent body she'd offered to him. "Who would have thought that I had scruples? And even a code of honor, warped as it is." He reached for the belt, cinching it tightly around her waist.

"Michael..."

"Shh. Don't say anything. I'm taking you home." He put a finger over her lips. "Don't look at me like that, Clemmie. I want you. Make no mistake about that. I want you more than you can imagine."

"Then why?"

"I won't take your innocence and leave you with nothing."

"What about what I want. I *need* you, Michael. I need you to make love to me."

"You need a good steady man who will take you to the altar and give you lots of children. I'm not the marrying kind."

"I know that, Michael. I've known it from the beginning."

"Knowing that, why did you offer yourself to me?"

She turned her back to him so he wouldn't see her face. She was afraid he would guess the truth. If he knew that she loved him, it would only add to his burden of— She searched her mind for the right word. Guilt? He had no reason to be guilty.

Trying to keep her love from showing, she turned back to him. "My life was so ordinary before you came along, so *scheduled*. Good heavens, I even had a routine for grocery shopping."

He smiled. "I remember."

"You changed that, Michael. You gave me excitement and glamour and romance." She folded her hands tightly together in front of her chest. "Peppertown is small. We don't get many strangers like you. You gave me a once-in-a-lifetime chance to know what it is like to be *intimate* with a handsome hero of a man."

"Clemmie...I hardly know what to say. You do me great honor."

He started to reach for her, then drew his hand back. He knew that if he touched her again, he wouldn't let go. He'd have what he'd wanted almost from the first day he'd seen her. What they both wanted, apparently. But tomorrow would come. It always did. And then she would hate him, for nothing would be any different. He'd told her the truth: he wasn't the marrying kind. And deep down, he sensed that she was. She was the kind of woman who needed a husband and children and a routine she could depend on.

"I have a confession to make," he continued. "When I came back to Peppertown, I had made a vow to myself to take you to my bed. I wanted to prove something—that you were an ordinary woman." His mouth turned up in the imitation of a rakish smile, but his eyes were sad. "You're no ordinary woman, Clemmie. I know that now, and that's partly the reason I can't make you a one-night stand."

"You're sweet, Michael. And I do understand what you're saying." She pressed her palms against her cheeks in frustration. "But I'm old enough to make my own mistakes and live with the consequences."

"I know you are. The simple truth is that this time I can't live with the consequences."

A silence descended on them as they gazed at each other and dreamed of what might have been. The storm outside, having spent its fury, sighed and swooned around the trailer, singing a death knell for the romance that never had a chance to happen.

Clemmie was the first to break the silence.

"You can take me back to my car now."

"Clemmie..."

"Yes?"

"I'll be in Peppertown at least five more weeks."

"I know."

"I can't let this situation between us get out of control again."

She watched him, waiting for him to explain.

"If you want to come back...to watch the filming..."

"I do."

"You're sure?"

She managed a small laugh. "Michael, there's an old saying about not cutting off your nose to spite your face. I like you. I want to see you. If I let what happened between us tonight stop me, I'd only be punishing myself."

At that moment Michael knew that somewhere, somehow, someone was watching over him. No man should be as lucky as he—to turn down a wonderful woman and still have her want to see him. He knew that seeing her again would be agony, but not seeing her would be hell.

He smiled.

"I'll call Bobo to follow us home."

Chapter Nine

Clemmie's protests that she could drive home herself had not done her one bit of good. Michael had called one of the actors, Lonnie Bobo, who had left a winning hand in poker for the chance to follow the famous couple home.

The windshield wipers on Clemmie's car made quiet swishing sounds. Still wearing Michael's green bathrobe, she sat in her corner of the car while he drove. Two skinny people could have sat in the space between them. By mutual consent, they did not touch.

The silence vibrated with forbidden feelings and unspoken thoughts. Clemmie wanted to capture time in a bottle. She wanted to preserve this last moment of intimacy so that she could savor it in the long, uneventful succession of the days of her life. Michael wished that he could change the past. He wished for a normal family where love was not a foreign word. He even went so far as to wish he had spent his adult years in honorable celibacy. Glancing at Clemmie, hugging the robe to herself in the darkness, he decided that the two saddest words in the English language were "if only."

The silence pressed down on Clemmie until she could no longer stand it. With the memory of Michael's touch still burning through her mind, she couldn't think of a thing to say, but *anything* would be better than this explosive silence.

"I can't believe Lonnie is still wearing that monster suit," she said.

Michael glanced in the rearview mirror at the set of headlights following them. Looking at Bobo was not as satisfying as looking at Clemmie, but it was a damned sight safer.

"Bobo is an actor through and through. He's starred in several of my pictures. I tell him he's more interested in his costume than in his salary."

"It was nice of him to come out in the rain like this."

"Bobo's a great guy and a good friend."

Small talk. For the first time in his life Michael was grateful for it. And he knew why they were doing it. Neither of them wanted to think about what had happened in the trailer.

"You're lucky to have a friend like him."

"Yes."

They lapsed into silence again. The steady slapping of the windshield wipers suddenly seemed loud. Clemmie pulled the robe closer around her neck and stared out the window.

Something crumbled inside Michael. Reaching across the seat, he took her hand.

"Clemmie?"

She turned to face him. In the dull glow of the dashboard lights her expression was tense.

"I'm sorry, Clemmie." He squeezed her hand.

"Don't be."

He knew he should probably let go of her hand, but he couldn't. It provided one last small contact with the woman he longed for but couldn't have. Keeping a tight hold, he turned into her driveway.

Lonnie Bobo pulled in behind them and hopped out of Michael's rental car. Dressed in his scaly green monster suit, he was oblivious of the rain.

Michael helped Clemmie from the car, shielding her from the rain with his black umbrella.

"Both of you are kind to escort me home." Clemmie smiled up at the friendly green monster. "Come inside for a cup of hot chocolate before you go."

Michael would have said no, for he needed to go back to the solitude of his trailer so he could think. But Lonnie was a social creature, a lover of parties, impromptu and planned, and a great fan of the human race in general. Clemmie, in particular, interested him. He had never met a woman who had so completely captured his imagination. He'd watched her on the set. He'd seen her charm, her kindness, and the way she'd had Michael under her spell. He wanted to go inside and find out if she was for real.

"Hot chocolate sounds great," he said.

The three of them went inside the boarding house.

"I'll get the milk heating. You can hang your wet things here in the hall." Clemmie went into the kitchen.

Michael hung his umbrella and rain slicker on the hall tree while Bobo surveyed the hallway, turning carefully so his long, scaly tail wouldn't knock against any furniture.

"Nice," he said. "Faded elegance." His voice was muffled by the wide, toothy snout.

At that moment Miss Josephine stuck her head around the parlor door. Seeing the monster she let out a yell. Before Michael could explain that the creature in her hallway was an actor in costume, she marched through the door, grabbed Michael's umbrella, and whacked Bobo's snout.

"Take that, you big bully." She flailed the umbrella over his head. "And that." Hopping around like a spry little sparrow, she began to rain earnest blows on the monster's tail. "Think you can scare folks in Peppertown, do you? Well, you have another thought coming."

By this time Michael was too entranced by the chemistry between Miss Josephine and the monster to do anything except watch. Bobo's thick scaly suit was more than enough protection from the frail old lady with the umbrella, and he was having the time of his life. He was hamming it up, howling in mock fear and rage, jumping around in his best creature-of-the-deep manner.

Clemmie hadn't known what to expect when she heard Miss Josephine scream, but she certainly hadn't expected to see Michael leaning against the wall, laughing.

"Good grief," she said as she hurried toward the old lady. "Miss Josephine! *Miss Josephine!*"

Oblivious to the shouting, Miss Josephine kept whacking away at the fearsome creature who had invaded her quiet home. Clemmie grabbed her arm.

"It's not a monster, Miss Josephine."

"I know it's not a lobster." The old lady lowered her umbrella long enough to face Clemmie. "It's a terrible monster. Stand back. I'll save you."

Clemmie shot a glance at Michael. "Do something."

He approached the old lady, lifted her off the floor, and carried her into the parlor, umbrella and all.

"The monster is a movie actor. *Movies!*" he shouted into her ear as he placed her on the sofa.

"Movies?" Miss Josephine gave him a bright smile and tucked a strand of hair behind her ear. "You want me to be in the movies?" She straightened the skirt of her print cotton dress. "Well, I don't mind if I do."

"Goodness gracious. What will we do now?" Clemmie turned as naturally to Michael as if she had been consulting him on important matters for years. "I don't know if I can ever make her understand."

Michael smiled at her. "You don't have to. What happened between her and Bobo was pure magic—a filmmaker's dream. If you think she's up to it, I'd like to have a small part written into the movie for her. It will be a great touch of humor and humanity."

"You'd really do that, Michael?"

"Yes."

Bobo, standing unnoticed beside the fireplace, didn't miss the looks that passed between those two. He'd already wagered a substantial amount that the unorthodox couple would end up at the altar. He was pleased to see things looking so promising.

"Thank you, Michael."

"You're more than welcome, Clemmie."

Bobo grinned. It had been a hell of a night to come out into the rain, but he'd done it partially to protect his investment. Judging by those suggestive grins, he would not be disappointed. In fact, he might even add a little to his wager.

Clemmie moved to the sofa and took the old lady's hand. "Miss Josephine, you're going to be a movie star."

"Wait till I tell Junior Wade about this."

"Who's Junior Wade?" Bobo asked.

Clemmie smiled at him. "If you have about an hour, we'll tell you over a cup of hot chocolate."

Bobo took off the head and tail of his costume while Clemmie brought a tray from the kitchen. The four of them toasted Miss Josephine's success with hot chocolate.

The next morning flowers arrived—orchids for Clemmie and roses for Miss Josephine. Tucked into the orchids was another of Shakespeare's sonnets. Michael's note to Miss Josephine was one of congratulations to his latest discovery.

He called at noon to tell Clemmie about the part that was being written for her spunky boarder.

"It's small, but it will require her to be on the set for a few days."

"That's no problem. I can bring her."

"You're sure? I can send a driver."

"She'll feel better with me. I'm familiar to her." Clemmie clutched the receiver to her ear and listened to the silence on the other end of the line. *Don't say no,* she thought to herself. *Give me this one last chance to be with you, even if it's only at a distance.*

"Clemmie . . . I'll look forward to seeing you on Monday."

The flowers got Clemmie through the weekend. Their fragrance sweetened the house and their beauty brightened her shabby rooms in a way that even a fresh coat of paint could not. Looking at them each day, she could almost feel Michael's presence.

When Monday finally came, she was breathless with anticipation. After much ado, she got Miss Josephine dressed and into the car. They saw the other boarders as they drove past Woody's Cafe.

Clemmie waved at them. "Looks like the school-teachers are back."

"I don't like black. Makes me look like a crow. If they bring out a black dress, I'm not wearin' it."

"It's Glen," Clemmie shouted, "and the rest of the teachers. They're back from their mini-sabbatical—that conference in St. Louis."

"No, I never knew Louis. Junior was my only lover."

Clemmie gave up. She had other things to think about, anyhow. What she would say to Michael? What he would say to her? What they would do? She knew it wouldn't be the same as last time, but still . . . seeing Michael was always so *exciting*.

Her heart set up a nervous trip-hammer rhythm as she turned the car into the gravel that had been hauled into the pasture over the weekend to keep cars from getting stuck in the mud.

Rick Love met them at the car. Clemmie tried to keep her disappointment from showing.

Rick helped Miss Josephine from the car. "I've been looking forward to meeting you. I'm Rick Love, the director."

"I never make love on the first date, young man. You've got the wrong woman."

Rick arched one eyebrow at Clemmie and grinned.

"Don't look at me," she said. "This was Michael's idea." She swung her head around, searching the set. "By the way, is he here today?"

"He and Jay went into Tupelo. A press conference, I believe."

"Oh." Clemmie tried to hide her disappointment, but it showed on her face.

Rick was quick to notice. When he'd first heard of Michael's intentions to court this woman publicly, he'd thought it was a publicity stunt. After meeting Clemmie, he'd changed his mind. There was something so warm and natural about her that it would be impossible not to respond. And Michael had. He'd seen it.

"I'm going to take good care of you today," he told Clemmie. As he escorted them to wardrobe for Miss Josephine's fitting he decided there was more to the romance than Michael was telling. And he was glad. He liked happy endings—in real life as well as in the movies.

"Watch your step. It's muddy around here since the rain." He helped Clemmie get Miss Josephine safely up the steps of the wardrobe trailer. "When you've finished here, I'll be back to take you to lunch."

Miss Josephine patted his cheek. "You're a nice young man. Unfortunately my hand is spoken for." She swept into the trailer as if she were born to be a movie star. "Young woman," she said to the wardrobe mistress, "I want to wear something sexy. And don't you dare put me in black."

Maria Trivoli, the head of wardrobe, was accustomed to dealing with all sorts of eccentric and egotistical people. She smiled at the old lady, introduced herself, and set about making the next two hours one of the best times Miss Josephine had ever had.

Clemmie thoroughly enjoyed the fitting. When she saw Rick she was going to tell him so. She'd rather have told Michael, of course, but it seemed that she would never get that chance.

Time passed so quickly that Clemmie was startled when the trailer door opened. Smiling, she started toward the door.

"Rick, it's been..." Words died in her throat and her hand flew to her mouth. The man standing in the door was not Rick Love.

"Hello, Clemmie."

Backlit by the sun, Michael Forrest looked like a god down from Mount Olympus. One of the handsome, golden ones. One of the sexy ones.

He smiled. "Sorry to disappoint you."

"You didn't disappoint me. You surprised me." *And thrilled me,* she wanted to say. "I was expecting Rick."

"I know. We finished the press conference sooner than I expected." He stepped into the trailer and shut the door behind him. "I thought I would check to see how Miss Josephine was doing." His gaze never left Clemmie. Seeing her was like standing in front of a fresh ocean breeze. He felt invigorated, alive, excited, and refreshed. Today she was wearing a soft pink sweater that made him want to taste her. But then, he always wanted to taste her, no matter what she was wearing. He backed against the door to keep from following through on his impulse.

"She's doing fine." Clemmie put her hands in the pockets of her corduroy skirt to keep from reaching toward Michael. Always, when she first saw him, she wanted to touch him. "She loves the red dress Maria is making for her. Michael..." She pulled one of her hands out of the pocket, then self-consciously put it back.

He leaned toward her. "Yes?"

The ache to touch and be touched quivered in the air between them. Clemmie took a deep breath, turning her eyes away from Michael so she could think straight.

"Today has been wonderful—for me as well as for Miss Josephine. I want you to know that." A flush colored her cheeks when she looked back at him. "You've given us something we would never have had without you.''

''And that is . . .''

''Excitement. Glamour.''

He didn't know why he was disappointed. What had he hoped she would say? Love? He chided himself for a fool.

''I'm glad. Can you stay for lunch?''

''If Miss Josephine is not too tired.''

He watched her consult Miss Josephine. It took five minutes to make the old lady understand. Michael marveled at Clemmie's patience. Her compassion, too. It was obvious to him that she was fond of Miss Josephine. He found himself almost envying the attention Clemmie lavished on her boarder.

When the matter of lunch was finally settled, Michael took Miss Josephine's arm and escorted them to the dining tent. Every step he took heightened his awareness of Clemmie. It didn't matter that the little old lady was between them. His blood sang with the nearness of Clemmie.

Their table was set with fresh flowers. On impulse he'd stopped at a florist in Tupelo and brought them back to Peppertown. When the three of them were settled at the table with steaming plates of food, he signaled to Lonnie Bobo. The multi-talented actor came over and serenaded them with his violin.

''This is enchanting,'' Clemmie said. *I love you*, her eyes told him.

''I thought Miss Josephine would like it,'' Michael replied. *I wanted you to have music*, his heart said.

Around them, the movie company watched. Not a single person believed that Michael Forrest had arranged flowers and music for Miss Josephine's benefit.

They knew he was courting Clementine Brady. The intriguing thing was that they didn't know what the outcome would be.

Rick and Jay, sitting across the tent from them, decided that *this time*, Michael had met a woman who was right for him. They just hoped he found it out before it was too late.

Lonnie Bobo, playing his violin, thought that sometimes real life was more fun than the movies.

The next few weeks passed in a blur for Clemmie. Her days were defined by flowers—roses on weekdays, orchids on the weekend. All from Michael. He was unfailingly generous and thoughtful. And he was always distant.

On the movie set, while Miss Josephine did her bit part, Clemmie sat in a special chair, a comfortable director's chair placed close enough to the action so that she could be there if Miss Josephine needed her. Michael was always there. He smiled at her when she arrived, greeted her briefly and politely, then disappeared to whatever chore called to him, usually something as far removed from her as possible. But she could feel him watching her. Sometimes when she looked up, she'd catch his eye. There would be a brief shining on his face, and then he'd turn away.

He kept his distance and he kept his vow: she would never be a one-night stand for Michael Forrest. It was just as well, she decided as she drove Miss Josephine home on the final day of her filming. Some women weren't cut out to be one-night stands, and she was one of them. For one thing, she wouldn't even know how to act. Would you say "Thank you," and politely leave after it was all over? Or would you kiss passionately and pretend it would never end, then go home and cry quietly into your pillow?

She didn't know, and now she never would. The brilliant days of October had given way to the apple crisp days of November, and soon Michael would be leaving. All she'd have would be the memories of a beautiful courtship and the sure knowledge that she loved him.

She turned her head so she could look at the movie set one last time. Michael was standing in the glow of sunset, watching her leave. He lifted his hand, and that was Clemmie's goodbye. She knew that as surely as she knew her name. He'd discovered scruples, he'd said. He wouldn't touch her again, wouldn't hold her so close that their heartbeats felt like one, wouldn't kiss her until she thought she'd fall off the edge of the earth. Never.

She hoped she could wait until she got home before the tears came.

"Well, if you ask me, somebody ought to give a party."

"What?" She'd been so busy with her own thoughts she'd been ignoring Miss Josephine.

"A party. For me. After all, I'm a movie star now."

"That's a great idea, Miss Josephine. David and Daniel are coming home on Thanksgiving weekend. It will be a perfect time for a celebration."

Celebrations and partings. How often were they intertwined? She'd think about that tomorrow, she decided as her Victorian house came into view. She'd think about a lot of things tomorrow.

Michael watched until Clemmie's car was out of sight. He was reminded of the time when he'd been eight. His neighbor had gotten a cocker spaniel for Christmas. Michael, who had never been allowed to have a dog because it might dig in the yard or mess up the furniture, had been given permission to go next door and play with the dog. Roger was the dog's name, a sturdy no-nonsense name for a spunky little animal who was all warm fur and wagging tail and wet tongue. Michael had spend six glorious weeks going next door every afternoon, playing with Roger.

One day when he'd crossed the hedge that separated their yards, he'd found the place deserted. No matter how loud he had called, Roger had not come. Finally an old man with a severe expression on his face had come out of the house and told him to shut up, that Roger had moved away and would never come when he called.

Fighting back the tears, for he'd been told that big boys didn't cry, he'd turned and gone bravely back to his own lonesome house. He felt that way now. But big boys didn't cry. And they certainly didn't hold up million-dollar pictures while they bemoaned the sorry state of their lives.

Resolutely he turned back to the set.

He left Peppertown six days later.

He'd watched a crew strike the set, supervised the loading of the heavy, expensive cameras, and watched the caravan of trucks and trailers pull out of the pasture that had been their home for the last few weeks.

It was over. Soon Peppertown would be just a memory, another footnote in the mental scrapbook of his life. The rental car slowed as he drove past a big white Victorian house. He hadn't meant to slow down, and he certainly hadn't meant to look. Partings were best done quickly. Prolonged goodbyes only added to the pain.

Clemmie was in her yard, gathering roses from a late-blooming bush beside the front door. The sound of his car must have alerted her, for she straightened up, shading her eyes against the sun, and looked right at him.

He couldn't drive past her. Cursing his own weakness, he pulled into her yard and cut the engine. She stood, clutching a rose against her chest.

The slamming of the car door sounded loud in the quiet November morning. Michael walked over to where Clementine stood.

"I didn't mean to come, Clemmie," he said when he stopped. "But when I saw you, I knew I couldn't leave without saying goodbye."

"You're leaving?"

"Yes. Today."

"I knew it would be soon, but I never dreamed..."

"What, Clemmie?"

"That I would be so unprepared for it." She reached hesitantly toward him, as if she weren't sure of her welcome.

He caught her hand and squeezed. "You have been a breath of fresh air in my life, sweet one."

"And you've been the best time I've ever known."

They clung to each other. Although nothing touched except their hands, they both had the sensation of being held heart to heart, touching length to length.

"Have I truly, Clemmie?"

"Yes. You've given me music and laughter and wine and roses." *And love,* she wanted to say. Instead she handed him the white rose, freshly cut from the bush. "A memento, Michael. Something to remember me by."

"Thank you, Clemmie." As he took the rose from her hand, he knew he would need no reminders of this woman. She was forever engraved on his heart. He gazed at her a while longer, thinking of all the things he wanted to say. In the end he said only one word. "Goodbye." Turning quickly, he strode back to his car.

"Take care, Michael."

Her parting words were still echoing in his mind when he arrived at the Tupelo Airport. Jay Wilkins, Rick Love and Lonnie Bobo were waiting for him. By the time he boarded the small jet that would take him to Memphis and his connecting flight, he knew he was leaving the best thing that had ever happened to him. He half rose from his seat.

Rick leaned across the aisle toward him. "Forget something, Michael?"

"Nothing. I'm just restless. Finishing a movie always does that to me."

"Yeah. I know the feeling—finish one thing and I can't wait to move on to another. What's your next project, Michael?"

"I think I'll look into that script Nikki Mackenzie sent me."

"I thought you said you weren't interested in doing a ghost story in Spain?"

Michael looked out the window. The city of Tupelo was a tiny toy town, boxed by cultivated fields and wrapped with highway ribbons. Somewhere east, just off Highway 78, was Peppertown. If he looked long enough, he might see a tiny white speck that was a Victorian house. Clemmie's house.

He turned back to Rick. "Spain suddenly holds a great appeal for me. It will do me good to get out of the country for a while."

"That bad, huh?"

"What do you mean?"

"It's called escape—putting an ocean between you and Clemmie."

"It's called business." He snapped open his briefcase and took out his appointment book. On page ninety-nine, pressed between Thanksgiving and Friday the twenty-fifth, was a single white rose. He used his index finger to trace the petals.

Chapter Ten

Daniel and David Brady arrived in Peppertown on Wednesday afternoon. They entered the big white boarding house like a parade, feet drumming on the hardwood floor, door banging on its hinges, deep bass voices sounding the trumpet call for their sister.

"Clemmie! We're home."

Clemmie was in the attic, striving to make a lump of clay resemble a bulldog, Mississippi State University's mascot. The pottery dog was going to be a Christmas gift for David. Oblivious to the commotion downstairs, she took a fresh lump of clay and added it to the snout. What she had now was an elephant, she decided. And that was nobody's mascot.

She squashed the clay with the flat of her hand and started over. Nothing she did these days seemed to turn out right. Michael had been gone for a little over a week, and she still hadn't adjusted. She burned two pans of gingerbread boys, made a batch of French pastry that didn't rise, stitched the sleeves in Daniel's Christmas shirt backward, and typed the wrong date on all the church bulletins. Reading Shakespeare made her sad and hearing *La Traviata* made her cry. She was going to have to do something about herself—and soon.

"Clemmie? Are you up here?"

She threw the lump of clay onto her hobby table and raced toward the door. "Daniel! David!" She was scooped off her feet by four brawny arms. Her twin brothers, laughing and jostling each other, made a pack saddle with their intertwined arms, and put Clemmie in the seat of honor.

"Put me down, you crazy things." Tears of joy ran down Clemmie's cheeks, and she didn't mean a word she said.

Her brothers ignored her commands, anyhow, just as they had been ignoring them for the last five years. They called it independence and she called it stubbornness.

"You're going to break your legs," she admonished as the two strapping young men carried her down the stairs.

"You've told us that a hundred times—every time we climbed a tree." Daniel winked across the top of her head at David.

"It wasn't the tree I was worried about; it was the garage roof." The boys had been in the house only two minutes, and Clemmie felt better already. She had missed them so!

"How about all those times she told us we'd catch pneumonia if we didn't put on our boots and gloves?" David chimed in.

"Yeah. She's a regular old worrywart."

Clemmie put her arms around their necks and hugged them close. "How have I managed without you two?"

"By the skin of your teeth, I guess." Daniel hooked a kitchen chair with his foot, dumped Clemmie onto its seat, then began to prowl through the cabinets. "I'm starved."

"You always are. Look on the top shelf of the pantry. I made some brownies this morning." She smiled as her brothers got a handful and began eating as if they hadn't had a meal in three days. "So, tell me about school."

"It's great, except for one thing—David's got all the women chasing him. That leaves me with zip."

"How about that hot little number who keeps calling you in the middle of the night?"

"You call ten o'clock the middle of the night?"

"It is when you're trying to sleep."

Smiling, Clemmie listened to the good-natured teasing of her brothers. They were exactly what she needed to cure the blues.

Daniel dragged a chair out from the table and straddled it. "So, big Sis, tell me about the movies."

The change of subject caught her off guard. "The movies?"

"Yeah," David said. "You wrote us about that big Hollywood producer who came to Peppertown. He sounded cool."

She knew that in teenage vernacular *cool* was a supreme compliment, but it was hardly the word she would have chosen to describe Michael. *Hot* was more appropriate. Even now, sitting in her kitchen with the brisk November winds blowing outside her windows, she felt hot just thinking about Michael Forrest.

"He was cool. As a matter of fact, he was wonderful." She didn't see the look David and Daniel exchanged. "While he was here, I got to visit the movie set and watch the filming."

"What was the movie called?"

"Don't talk with food in your mouth, David." He rolled his eyes toward the ceiling. "*Moonlight Madness*. Michael even had a part written for Miss Josephine."

"Michael?"

"The movie producer, knucklehead. Don't you remember Clemmie's letter? Jeez! No wonder all the women chase me. I'm the one with brains." David ate the rest of his brownie and even wiped the chocolate off his mouth before he spoke again. "So... will we get to meet the hotshot or what?"

"No. He's gone back to L.A."

Clemmie thought she was hiding her heartbreak well, but her twin brothers, ever attuned to the person they loved best in the world, saw the longing in her face. Daniel, who had been born two minutes earlier than his twin and prided himself on being the oldest, signaled to his brother.

"Back in a minute, Clemmie," he said as he dragged David out into the hallway.

Clemmie was used to the abrupt appearances and departures of teenagers. Instead of wondering what was going on, she rose from her chair and opened the refrigerator. She punched the turkey to see if it would be thawed for tomorrow's Thanksgiving dinner. This was her brothers' first visit home since the beginning of the semester, and she wanted everything to be perfect.

She was still testing the turkey when David and Daniel came back into the room.

Daniel took her arm. "Can we have a serious talk, Sis?"

"Of course. It's not school, is it? I thought you both were doing fine."

"No. It's not school."

"It's the flowers," David blurted.

"What flowers?" Clemmie sat back down in her chair.

Behind her back, Daniel made a slashing motion across his throat, then pulled out a chair. This time he sat properly in the seat.

"We saw all those vases of dead flowers in the hallway and the parlor when we came in. One of the cards was still on the hall table. It said *Michael*."

"Yeah." David scooted his chair closer to Clemmie. "Now, before you go trying to act like we're still thirteen and you're the mama, we want to know how come you looked so sad when we mentioned that dude's name and why you kept all those dead flowers? If you're upset about something, we want to know. Maybe we can help you for once."

Daniel took her hand. "It's because we love you. And it's high time we grew up and started taking some of the responsibility around here."

Clemmie glanced from one brother to the other. What they had said was true. They weren't thirteen anymore. The three months they'd been at college, their shoulders had broadened, their faces had matured, and they had grown half an inch taller. What was more, they were offering to share a part of her life.

"How sweet of both of you." She smiled at them. "I'm afraid there's nothing you can do about this problem. I simply fell in love with the wrong man."

David and Daniel sat back in their chairs, astonished. Love was one of those words that got bandied about a lot on the college campus, but nobody took it seriously. And yet, here was their sister, the epitome of responsibility, saying that she had fallen in love.

Daniel was the first to recover. "That's great, Sis. That you're in love, I mean."

"Yeah. He must have loved you, too, or he wouldn't have sent all those flowers."

Clemmie had to smile. They made love sound so simple. "He might have. I don't know. Love was something Michael and I never talked about."

"Why not?" This from the impulsive David.

"Because it wasn't appropriate. His work is in Hollywood and my responsibilities are here." She took their hands and squeezed. "Don't you two know that I would never abandon you?"

"Abandon us? Golly dang, Sis, David and I are grown. We can take care of ourselves."

"Even if Michael loved me—and I'm not saying he did—you two could never manage school and keeping the house."

"We can manage with our school loans and our after-school jobs. Anyhow, we love this house because you are here, Clemmie. Until we have families of our own, home is wherever you are."

"That's right," David added. "I think Hollywood would be neat."

Clemmie had always thought of her brothers as young boys who needed caring for. Now she was astonished at their grown-up wisdom.

"I'm proud of you," she said. "I never dreamed you'd feel this way. Anyhow, it's too late. Michael's in L.A. and I'm here, and that's that." She pushed back her chair and stood up. "Tonight we're having a party, just you and me and Miss Josephine and all the other boarders. It will be a celebration of your Thanksgiving homecoming."

Later, after finishing her discussion with her brothers, Clemmie set about making the house festive for the impromptu party, dragging out tinsel from last year's Christmas tree and draping it up the staircase banister. She sent David and Daniel to the grocery store for a supply of balloons. Harvey came home early, stowed his tuba in his room, and pitched in with the party preparations.

By eight o'clock that evening, the old boarding house looked like a cross between a Christmas pageant, a birthday party, and a Fourth of July picnic. Clemmie, her brothers and all her boarders were gathered in the parlor.

"I propose a toast to Miss Josephine, Peppertown's movie star." Clemmie lifted her glass of homemade wine. "Long may you shine."

A chorus of agreement filled the room.

"To Thanksgiving," Harvey said.

"To life," Miss Josephine added.

"To Clemmie." Daniel stepped away from the small gathering beside the sofa and took his sister's hand. "All of us here want to show our gratitude for the many ways you make our life comfortable and pleasant and easy. And so—" pausing dramatically, he reached into his pocket "—we're giving you this gift." He pulled out a one-way ticket to L.A.

Thanksgiving Day was like any other day to Michael. He worked. He'd given the butler, the cook, the maid, and the gardener the day off, of course, but he'd gone to his office as usual. The Spanish project was moving along as fast as he could push it. With each passing day, he felt an increasing urgency to leave the country.

He drove himself, poring relentlessly over scripts, watching screenings until he was bleary-eyed. When he finally left his office, he was so exhausted he had nothing on his mind except a quick shower, a frozen TV dinner, and bed. And he was glad. Exhaustion was the state he'd been striving for. It left him no energy to think.

The house looked quiet when he drove up, no lights, no barking dogs, no family to greet him at the door.

"Happy Thanksgiving," he muttered as he parked the car.

When he opened his front door, the first thing he noticed was the smell of roast turkey.

"What the hell?" He stood in his marble and tile hallway.

"Welcome home, Michael."

He heard her before he saw her. The soft Southern voice poured over him like a balm.

"Clemmie?"

Whirling around, he saw her, standing in the doorway, wreathed in a white apron and a smile. It was his cook's apron, and it was too big for Clemmie. The strings were wrapped twice around her small waist and the bib drooped over her chest. She had flour on her cheek and a shine in her eyes.

Michael stood in the hallway, mesmerized, hardly daring to believe his eyes.

"My brothers and my boarders took up a collection and bought me a ticket to Hollywood. They seemed to think I should come." Clemmie's cheeks flushed hot, and she knew she was babbling, but she didn't know what else to do. Michael had made no move toward her, and she couldn't tell what he was thinking. All the things she'd planned to say had departed her whirling brain. "I knew where you lived, of course. Your address was in my guest book. When I got to L.A., though, I was a little intimidated. I found Rick's phone number, and he met me at the airport. He got somebody to let me in your house. A man named Greaser Johnson, I believe."

"Rick and I met him at one of my parties. He was upstairs going through my female guests' purses. He's a cat burglar."

"Good grief. You mean I consorted with a criminal?"

Michael smiled. "Still the same innocent Clemmie. Your reputation is intact, my sweet. He's reformed now. Straight as an arrow . . . except when somebody like Rick talks him into straying."

Now that they had exhausted the subject of how she had come and how she had gotten into his house, neither of them knew what to say. Clemmie pressed her palms together, waiting for some sign from Michael— welcome, rejection, anything. He was so still he barely seemed to be breathing. His expression was fierce, and he studied her until she grew almost faint from nerves.

Finally he spoke. "I noticed you have a soft spot for strays. Is this a charity visit, Clemmie?"

Heaven help me to know what to do, she thought. She certainly couldn't blurt out that she loved him, not with him looking as remote as Alaska.

"No. It's not a charity visit. Call it friendship."

"Do you have a place to stay?"

"No."

A breathless silence descended on them once more. It stretched out until Clemmie's nerves were twanging. She reached up and pushed her hair back from her face.

Something snapped in Michael. He moved swiftly across the tiled floor. When he was only inches from Clemmie he stopped.

"You have flour on your face."

"Oh?" Her hand fluttered upward.

He caught her hand. "When you pushed your hair back you smeared it across your cheek." Releasing her hand, he reached up and gently rubbed her cheek. "Here." His fingers lingered, caressing the soft skin he'd dreamed about for almost two hellish weeks. "That should take care of it."

"Thank you," she whispered.

"You're welcome." With desire and need screaming along his nerve endings, he stepped back. "You can stay here."

"You're sure? I don't want to be a bother."

"The house is big. Nobody will bother you."

She wept inside. This conversation wasn't at all the way she had imagined. Thirty thousand feet in the air she'd dreamed of a different welcome, of Michael opening his arms and his heart to her. Now it seemed that nothing had changed. Neither distance nor time had made him more receptive to love. She should never have come to Hollywood. There was nothing to do but make the best of a bad decision.

She turned up the corners of her mouth in the imitation of a bright smile. "That's very generous of you. I'll leave first thing in the morning."

"No." He hadn't realize he'd spoken so harshly until she flinched. Cursing himself, cursing the fates, he softened his voice. "You can stay as long as you like. My friends are always welcome here."

"I'll think about that tomorrow. Right now, why don't we eat the turkey?"

"Is that what I smelled when I came in the house?"

"Yes. I talked Rick into helping me buy a few groceries. Your pantry was almost empty."

His laughter was genuine. For the first time since he'd entered his house, he relaxed.

"Still pampering everybody in sight, aren't you, Clementine Brady?"

"A body has to eat, and I do love cooking. Anyhow, it's Thanksgiving."

"I never knew it was until you walked through my door." He draped an arm across her shoulders and led her toward the kitchen. "This house has never smelled so good. Do you mind if I stick my nose in a few pots and pans?''

"I'd love it." Clemmie's mother had once told her the way to a man's heart was through his stomach. Watching Michael now, she almost believed it. "Your kitchen is beautifully equipped, Michael. I took a few liberties when I was searching for pots and pans."

Everything in his kitchen was state of the art, but today was the first time it had ever smelled and felt so homey. Michael replaced the lid on a pot of giblet gravy and smiled at Clemmie.

"Coming here was dangerous, you know."

"Dangerous?"

"I'm liable to keep you out here..." The lovely look of expectation on her face twisted his gut. "...to cook." Right now, cooking was the last thing on his mind, but he didn't want to give her any false impressions. In spite of the way he felt with her in his house, he had not changed his mind. He was what he was, and he couldn't change that overnight. Clemmie deserved more.

Standing in his kitchen, surrounded by the smells of Thanksgiving, he hungered for her. He hoped his new-found nobility would hold up under the tension of this unexpected visit. Hell. Looking at her now, with her ripe lips and ripe body, he hoped his nobility would last through the evening meal. What he wanted to do was back her up against the kitchen counter and love her until they were both panting.

Clemmie rescued him.

"Your house is beautiful...the parts Rick showed me. That mahogany table in your dining room is especially lovely. I wonder if we might use it tonight? We can make this a very festive occasion."

"With you, Clemmie, every moment is a festive occasion." He loved the way she flushed at his remark. Too much. He loved it too much. "I'll set the table." He hurried to the dining room and flung open his china cabinet. The Baccarat crystal and Limoges china rattled on the shelves. He handled the expensive glassware as if it were cheap dime-store plastic. Nothing mattered to him except the woman standing in his kitchen. An alarming thought. He'd have to do better than that or he would never make it through the night.

He made it through the meal. As a matter of fact, he enjoyed the meal so much that he was reluctant to leave the table. He guessed Clemmie must be a mind reader, for she kept the conversation light. Nothing personal, no reminders of those steamy nights in Mississippi when he'd come so close to robbing her of her virginity. He was relieved . . . and grateful.

"Clemmie, you don't know what this means to me. I can't believe you left your home to spend Thanksgiving here."

"As I said, the one-way ticket was a gift."

"One way?"

She tried to cover the slip. "You can imagine my surprise when David and Daniel gave it to me. I had planned a big dinner for the boarding house. In fact, the turkey was already thawing. But everybody was so pleased about what they had done. Naturally I couldn't refuse the gift."

"Naturally."

She'd come to him on a one-way ticket. What was her reason? he wondered. The possibilities boggled his mind. And he discovered that he was much too tired to think about them tonight.

"Clemmie, would you like to see L.A. by night?"

"That would be wonderful. But the dishes—"

"They can wait. The maid will be back tomorrow." He saw the struggle she had with her conscience about leaving dirty dishes on the table, even if the maid was coming the next day. "Humor me, love," he said lightly.

She did. She walked blithely out the door and left the clean-up job for somebody else. It felt good for once.

"Of course, I wouldn't want to make a habit of this," she told Michael as he helped her into her lightweight coat.

He grinned. "Of course not."

There were three cars in Michael's garage—a Silver Cloud Rolls-Royce, a Jaguar, and a Toyota pickup truck. He chose the Jag for their outing.

As he drove through Hollywood Hills he felt as if he were seeing his neighborhood for the first time. Clemmie's approach to sightseeing was the same as her approach to life: she discovered something to love at every turn, and she tried to make every minute count.

She thought all the houses hanging on the side of the Santa Monica mountains were fabulous.

"Your home is the most wonderful, of course," she said.

He'd never thought of his home as wonderful. It was well-built, architecturally pleasing, and functional.

"Why is that?"

"It's friendly."

"Friendly?"

"Yes. That grand courtyard and that fabulous greenhouse just hold their arms out in welcome. Don't you feel it, Michael?"

"Only since you came."

She pinned her hopes on that phrase... and on his smile. Across the other side of the car, he was smiling as he had in Peppertown, with joy and a certain dare-devil charm that gave her great pleasure. She leaned her head against the plush leather seat and sighed.

"Tired?"

"No. Blissful."

Michael thought of her one-way ticket again. Since it was dark and he was driving and couldn't do much with his hands even if he wanted to, he risked asking a loaded question.

"And what is the reason for your bliss?"

The comfortable darkness made her brave. "You, Michael."

They were headed northwest now, into the fertile San Fernando Valley. Michael drove awhile, thinking about what she had said. He didn't want to give her the wrong idea, but no answer at all seemed cruel. Abruptly he swung the car onto a small gravel road that led up into the mountains. He parked on a mountain overlook and cut the engine.

"I've never known a woman like you, Clemmie. You are totally unselfish . . ." He turned so he could see her. The moonlight slashed across her cheek and highlighted her vamp's mouth. "And far too desirable." He reached out and gently touched her cheek.

She covered his hand with her own. For her, it was all or nothing. She'd taken the risk of coming to Hollywood uninvited, and now it was time to take the final risk.

"I want you, too, Michael. But it's much more than desire, much more than need. When you first came to Peppertown, I saw you as my chance for excitement and glamour and even a taste of sex. The only problem was, you developed scruples . . . and I fell in love with you."

His hand trembled on her cheek. When he started to speak, she put her free hand over his lips. "Please don't say anything yet. Let me say what I have to say before I lose my courage."

"I'm listening, Clemmie."

"I didn't come out here for a ring or a wedding or even a commitment. I came merely to tell you that I love you. You're the best thing that's ever happened in my life, and I couldn't let you go without telling you exactly how I feel."

His hand left her cheek and caressed her lips. "I've dreamed of you every night. I've pictured you here in L.A., in my house, in my arms, in my bed. But there's always something wrong with the picture. An affair doesn't fit you, Clemmie. Even life in Hollywood doesn't seem right for you. You're too innocent, too natural, too *good*." He gave a rueful smile. "Although seeing you here does lead me to wonder if I've been wrong."

"I'll have an affair with you. I can get a job out here."

"What about your brothers? The boarding house?"

"My brothers have student loans. Those can be increased. Harvey's watching after the house now, and I can eventually find a buyer. And I'll find a good place for Miss Josephine. She has no one except me, you know."

Michael pulled her into his arms and pressed his face against her hair. "Ah, Clemmie, you tempt me so."

He held her that way for a while, tenderly, pressing her so close he could feel her heart beating against his chest. And he kept a tight rein on his passion.

Finally she lifted her head.

"Michael?"

"You wouldn't have to take a job. You wouldn't even have to sell your house. I'm a wealthy man, Clemmie. I can afford to support you and your brothers and Miss Josephine and keep all the houses in Mississippi you want." He gave her a smile, and she thought it was the saddest one she'd ever seen. "The answer is no, my sweet. I would never forgive myself if I made you a kept woman."

Burrowing her face into his chest, she hugged him tightly. "And I would never have forgiven myself if I hadn't tried."

Michael cupped her face. "Clemmie, don't ever settle for an affair...with anybody."

"I never thought I would. And perhaps, even with you, I wouldn't have—not for long. But loving you as I do, it seemed the best thing to say." She smiled at him. "Do you know that you really are a knight in shining armor, Michael Forrest?"

"Why do you say that?"

"You've rescued me from my own misguided intentions."

He started the car and headed back down the mountain to his home in Hollywood Hills.

It was past midnight when Clemmie went to bed. Michael had shown her into a guest room that was down the hall from his own bedroom. Actually it wasn't a room: it was a suite of rooms—a sitting room, bedroom and bath in luscious peach colors that made her feel pampered. She tried her best to hang on to that feeling— pampered. As long as she could concentrate on that, she could push aside her other feelings—defeat, disappointment, heartbreak.

Fastening her robe high around her neck, she sat down at the vanity and picked up her hairbrush. She always gave her hair one hundred stokes at night. The small routine was soothing.

Downstairs Michael sat in his leather chair and stared at the bookshelves along the wall of his den. He was a collector of books. He had some first editions of the greats—Herman Melville, Mark Twain, John Steinbeck. He had a few original letters of Cotton Mather and

Dashiell Hammett and some of the Mark Twain papers. His collection was the envy of bibliophiles for miles around.

Underneath his feet was an Oriental rug. The amount he'd paid for it would have put Clemmie's brothers through college. The furniture was Louis XIV, original, and his walls were hung with Matisse and Picasso.

For all the thought he gave his material possessions, he might as well have been sitting in a stable surrounded by hay and cows. His thoughts were centered on one woman—Clemmie. Right now she was upstairs in one of his guest bedrooms.

And she loved him.

The thought haunted him, taunted him and finally prodded him from his chair. He paced his room, a prisoner of his own thoughts. No matter what excuses he had made for holding back from Clemmie—calling himself a rake, a jaded Don Juan, a cynical reckless bachelor— he'd still been caught in her tender trap. And yet, now that she had come to Hollywood, he didn't feel trapped at all. Actually he felt a soaring freedom, as if he had been waiting all his life for this moment, for this woman who held the key to his prison.

What was he to do about it? Stopping by his liquor cabinet, he poured himself a good shot of scotch. He'd be going on location in Spain in another month if he pushed hard enough. Maybe he could just drift until then, let things take their natural course. She'd go back to Peppertown and forget about him. And what would he do? Keep on running?

The scotch burned his throat going down. Suddenly he saw Clemmie's face, heard her voice. "I came merely to tell you that I love you."

He set the glass on a table with such force the amber liquid sloshed onto the polished mahogany. Then he was off and running. He took the stairs two at a time. When he reached the end of the hallway, he had to stop and get his breath.

Praying for composure and the right words, he pushed open the door.

"Thank God you're wearing white cotton."

Clemmie was sitting beside the vanity brushing her hair, and her cheeks went bright pink when she looked up.

Michael laughed. "I feel like a fool."

"You look like a hero. Won't you come in?"

"I've been a perfect jackass, Clemmie. I probably should have stopped and given this some thought, but now that I'm here, I guess there's only one way to say it."

Her hand went to her throat. The gesture made Michael ache.

"I love you, Clemmie."

"Michael!"

He stood in the doorway, taking courage from the solid feel of his well-built house.

"I've loved you for a long, long time. It just took me awhile to admit it, even to myself."

Clemmie slowly put the hairbrush on the table and folded her hands in her lap. She was filled with such jubilation she could barely sit still, but she forced herself. She'd flown two thousand miles to declare her love for Michael and to find out how he felt about her. She wasn't about to spoil everything by a wrong move now.

He came toward her. When he was close enough, he knelt at her feet and took her hand. "I'm asking you to marry me, Clemmie."

"I've always wanted an old-fashioned proposal."

"Is that a yes?"

"Yes. Oh, yes, yes, yes."

She flung her arms around him and almost toppled them both to the floor. Michael steadied her, then stood up, pulling her into his arms.

Until that moment he hadn't believed it was possible for a man to feel such happiness. Holding Clemmie, he buried his face in her hair, absorbing the fragrance of her, the feel of her. A thousand years would not be enough time to show his love for this woman.

"Say yes again, Clemmie. I want to know that I heard you correctly."

She reached up and gently cupped his face. "Michael Forrest, I love you. It will give me great honor to be your wife."

"My wife...I like the sound of those words." He caught one of her hands and kissed the palm. As always, one taste of her was not enough. He fitted her arms around his neck and lowered his mouth to her. The kiss was heady with passion and rich with promise.

Groaning, he backed them toward the bed. The mattress squeaked under their weight. Clemmie's dark hair fanned against the covers. Propping himself on his elbows, Michael lifted the silken strands, letting them drift slowly through his fingers. "I've wanted you here, pictured you here...just like this."

"I'm here, Michael. I'm real." She pressed tender kisses around his jaw. "Love me."

"Ahh, Clemmie. You tempt me so." Careful not to put his entire weight on her, he pressed full length, feeling every soft curve and enticing hollow of her body. She was his. She'd given her promise. He exulted in the knowledge.

"Michael?"

"Hmm?" Almost drugged with the nearness of her, he looked down into her face.

"Is there any reason..." She hesitated, her smile so heart-breakingly innocent he wanted to shout his happiness for the whole world to hear. Licking her dry lips, she tried again. "Is there any reason to wait?"

His joy bubbled over. Laughing, he pulled her into a bear hug. "Treasures are always worth waiting for...but not too long." He sat up, taking her with him. "How do you feel about getting a license tomorrow?"

"If you hadn't suggested that, I was going to mention it myself."

Delight poured through him, shining on his heart and illuminating the dark corners of his soul. Clemmie. She was his Clemmie. She was his hearth, his home, his love. He'd wait, because he'd finally found a woman worth waiting for.

He brushed her tumbled hair back from her face and kissed her gently on the lips. "Good night, my darling."

"Good night, Michael."

Then he left her bedroom and firmly shut the door.

They got their blood tests, applied for their marriage license and were married by a cherub-faced justice of the peace. Michael took his bride back to his house immediately after the ceremony.

"Welcome home, Mrs. Forrest." She laughed when he carried her across the threshold.

"Is this going to be an old-fashioned, traditional marriage, Mr. Forrest?"

"Till death do us part, Mrs. Forrest. I intend to keep those vows."

He stepped into the hall and kicked the door shut.

"What do you intend to do about the loving and cherishing part?"

"If you can wait a little while longer..."

"Michael!"

"... till we get up the stairs."

"Only if you hurry."

And he did. Holding her in his arms, he hurried up the stairs.

He'd kept his vows. Clemmie had never been a one-night stand for him. Even after she'd said yes, he'd kept his passion in check. And now he carried his innocent bride into his bedroom.

He set her on her feet, but kept her close against his chest. "Clemmie, do you mind doing something for me?"

"Anything, Michael."

"I want to spend my wedding night with my bride in her white cotton gown."

She blushed. "The sun is shining. It's only two in the afternoon."

"My love, by the time we leave this bedroom, it will be night."

She disappeared into the dressing room, and when she came back she took his breath away. Her eyes were shining, her hair was gleaming, and she was dressed from head to toe in white cotton. No flesh showed except her face, her hands, the tips of her toes, and a slender band on her throat.

He walked slowly toward her. "'All my fortunes at thy foot I'll lay...'" Kneeling, he lifted one of her feet and kissed her toes.

Tingles of pleasure shot along her spine. As he picked up her other foot she finished the Shakespearean quotation he'd begun. "'...and follow thee, my lord, throughout the world.'"

He rose and took her hand. "Remember how it was with us, Clemmie? Even when we first met, I was courting you with Shakespeare." He pressed an urgent kiss into her damp palm. "If the old bard were here right now, what do you suppose he would say?"

"He'd probably say, "'Your wife loves you very much, Michael.'"

"Come here and show me, love." Pulling her into his arms, he began caressing her back. "I'll be gentle with you, my sweet."

He circled her mouth with his tongue, nibbled her lower lip, then took her in a full-bodied, heady kiss that made her go limp. She tangled her hands in his hair.

"Oh, Michael. Love me."

"Always . . ." He unfastened the top three buttons of her white cotton robe and placed his hand over her bare chest. Stretching his fingers, he brushed lightly against the tops of her breasts. ". . . and forever."

"I love you to touch me there, Michael. It feels . . ." She sucked in her breath as he pushed aside the soft fabric and cupped her bare breast.

"Tell me, sweet. Tell me how it feels."

"Like I am Earth Mother—" she tightened her hands in his hair and unconsciously pulled his head downward "—and all my life juices are outward flowing."

He buried his face in her neck, kissing the soft skin, pressing his tongue against the base of her throat to feel her pulse. It was wild and erratic.

"Relax, love." He slid her robe off her shoulders, and it fell at their feet. With the bright California sun slanting through the French windows, he could see her body through the thin cotton of her gown.

With an effort, he held onto his control. Today was the first day of the rest of their lives. What he did in this bedroom would determine how Clemmie viewed the physical side of their marriage.

While his mouth suckled her breasts, his hands carefully pulled the cotton gown upward to bare her buttocks. Clemmie moaned when he pulled her bare hips gently against his.

Blindly she reached for his belt buckle.

"That's right. Undress me." He steadied her hands as they fumbled with the zipper on his pants. "Feel me. Touch me." Murmuring words of encouragement, he helped her get his pants off.

He stood boldly in the sun, watching her eyes widen when she saw him. She reached for him, tentative and shy.

"Go ahead, sweet. Touch me." He guided her hand, closed it around himself.

"I never knew," she whispered.

"I'm glad." He groaned as her hand caressed him. "Oh, God, sweet. That's good."

Clemmie wet her lips with her tongue, hungry now for him, impatient. She unbuttoned his shirt and cast it aside. Her hand massaged his chest.

"I remember how this felt. So good, Michael." Leaning down she tasted the taut tanned skin over his breastbone. "So good."

"Ah, yes, Clemmie." He pulled her head closer. Her tongue wet his nipple. "Like that, my love."

Stepping back, her eyes blazing, she lifted her gown over her head. It fell to the floor in an innocent heap. With the natural ease of a sensuous woman, she arched her back and lifted her breasts to him.

"I'm yours, Michael. Love me."

He picked her up and carried her to the bed. Placing her in a patch of sunlight, he hovered over her. Her right hand slid along his body, nearly shattering his tight control.

"I want to know every inch of you, Clemmie, every soft curve and secret hollow." Leaning on one elbow, he began to trace her body with his hand. "After today, you will belong to me, my sweet. Only to me.'' Murmuring soft love words, he traced her breasts, her stomach, her legs. His voice was thick when he parted her thighs. She was ready for him. When his hand slipped inside, she gasped.

"I won't hurt you, love."

"No... I know that... oh, Michael..." Her hips began a small rhythm. "I need... I want..."

"Easy, love." He lifted himself over her. "Easy."

He slid into her, holding back for fear of hurting her. But she plunged against him, taking him fully. The brief resistance and her small cry of pleasure-pain were the only signs that she was an innocent woman. Ecstasy ripped through him.

"Did I hurt you?"

"No..." She clutched his back. "Love me, Michael."

And he did. There on his bed, in his home, he consummated their marriage. Loving Clemmie, he knew such joy he thought he would die. He held back, waiting, waiting until her cry of fulfillment rang out. Then he spilled his seed.

They didn't come out of the bedroom until eight o'clock the next morning. They were ravenous and euphoric. They ate a logger's breakfast and called Peppertown.

Daniel answered the phone.

"Clemmie, is that you?"

"Yes. It's me."

"My gosh. We've been waiting so long to hear from you. How are things going?"

"Splendid. Michael and I are married."

"Married?"

"Yes. We decided to have a quick wedding here in L.A. before heading back to Peppertown."

"You're coming here? *He's* coming here?"

Clemmie smiled and winked at her husband. "Of course. You didn't think I'd let my family miss my wedding, did you?"

"Your wedding? I thought you said you were already married."

"We are, legally. But both of us want a big wedding with family and friends. We're flying home at the end of next week."

After she had hung up, Michael pulled her into his arms. "How do you feel about love in a bubble bath, Mrs. Forrest?"

"I don't know. I've never tried it."

Laughing, he picked her up and carried her back up the stairs. "Mrs. Forrest, I intend for you to try everything ... with me."

They flew back to Peppertown eight days after their marriage in L.A. In that length of time, Michael had kept all the servants out of his house so he and his bride could honeymoon in secret; he had spent enough time on the phone to plan a wedding extravaganza in Peppertown, and he had finally called all his friends and invited them to his wedding—his *second* wedding.

"I figured I'd waited so long and been so scared of this, I might as well do it twice," he'd told Rick Love.

Now they were all assembled in Clemmie's yard—Rick Love, Jay Wilkins, Lonnie Bobo, Miss Josephine, Harvey, Glen and the other schoolteachers, David and Daniel—waiting for the bride and groom. A full orchestra was playing, the gazebo was draped with white roses and orchids, a white carpet was laid upon the browning grass, and the weather was cooperating beautifully. The temperature was a mild sixty-one, and the early December sun was outdoing itself with brilliance.

Spirits were high. And this crowd, loving a good show the way they did, was whispering and murmuring its pleasure. Suddenly a hush came over them.

A magnificent white stallion bearing two riders came into view. The saddle and bridle were the finest leather, trimmed with real gold. Riding double were Michael and Clemmie. He wore the loose white shirt, black pants and black boots of the buccaneer, and she was dressed in a fairy-tale wedding gown of white satin and tulle, trimmed with white sequined roses. They looked as if they had stepped straight from a lavish Cinderella castle.

And they almost had. The week in Michael's plush mansion in Hollywood Hills had made Clemmie feel almost like Cinderella. Almost, but not quite. Her head might have been in the clouds for a while, but she had her feet firmly planted on the ground. She was married to a real man, a prince, to be sure, but a man of flesh and blood and passion. And she planned to be married to him for the rest of her life.

She smiled as he helped her from the horse, and there beside her gazebo they pledged their vows a second time. It was a wedding to remember, with music that rivaled heaven's choirs, color photographs taken from every angle, a videotape made that would be shown over and over, well wishes of family and friends, and flowers to press in a scrapbook.

And when it was over, when the last crumb of cake had been eaten and the last glass of champagne drunk, all the guests slipped quietly away, leaving the Victorian house to the almost newlyweds.

Michael carried Clemmie over yet another threshold and up another set of stairs. The brass bed waited for them, the white sheets turned rosy by the glow of sunset that washed through the windows.

"Remember what you once told me about this brass bed, Clemmie?"

"Yes. From the first day you arrived in Peppertown I imagined us there, together."

"I love it when you blush." He cupped her cheek, pulling her close with gentle pressure. "Tell me, love, what did you imagine?"

She bent forward and whispered in his ear. He lifted one wicked eyebrow in mock surprise.

"No," he said, chuckling. "You don't mean it." Her face getting pinker and pinker, she continued to whisper. "Not that, too. Why, Mrs. Forrest, I'm positively delighted with you."

He unbuttoned her satin gown, slid it down and kissed her slim, firm shoulders. She shivered with pleasure.

"If we live to be a hundred, Michael, I will never get enough of you."

"Nor I of you." Taking her hand, he guided it across his chest and down the front of his body. "Feel how I want you, Clemmie. Just looking at you does this to me."

She chuckled. "Then I'll have to promise not to come to any of your board meetings."

"Come ahead. I'll dismiss the meeting."

She shrugged off her dress and stepped into his arms. "And then what will we do, Mr. Forrest?"

"I've always believed showing is better than telling."

The bedsprings squeaked as he lowered her to the sun-painted covers. She circled her arms around his neck and pulled him close. He slipped inside her, and it was as if they had always belonged together. They lay still a moment, savoring each other, building the anticipation.

"Do you know what Miss Josephine said the first day you came here?"

"Tell me, my sweet."

"She said you were a philandering man and we would all be pregnant as a house if you stayed."

He chuckled. "The first part is over and done with. But I think I can do something about the second part—" his hips began to move "—with you, my love. Only with you."

Epilogue

Michael parked his Jaguar and stopped by the greenhouse to pick a large red hibiscus. When he walked into the front hallway, he was attacked by three laughing children and two rowdy dogs.

"Daddy, Daddy! You're home." The four-year-old twins, Jimmy and Josie, vied with each other to see who could climb his legs the fastest.

Margaret, whose droopy diaper had slowed her down, pulled her thumb out of her mouth and gazed at him with solemn amber eyes. "Daddy's girl wants up."

He was lifting her into his arms when his wife appeared in the doorway. As always, his heart beat faster at the sight of her. She still had the refreshingly sexy look of an innocent vamp. And she still made him almost crazy with desire.

Clemmie took his arm and patted baby Margaret on the bottom at the same time. "She has you wrapped around her finger."

"What can I say? You know how two-year-olds are."

She leaned around Margaret's tousled golden curls to give her husband a kiss.

"Well, are you two going to kiss all day or are we flying to Peppertown?"

Michael and Clemmie kissed awhile longer, for they knew that Miss Josephine loved nothing more than a bit of romance. When they broke apart, they looked at her. She was holding onto the twins' hands and wearing her sprigged muslin dress and her dead corsage. Each year they marveled that she was still with them. She seemed to get younger instead of older. She swore that getting to do occasional bit parts in Michael's movies was better than finding the fountain of youth.

"We're going to the airport as soon as Michael can get the car loaded. Thanksgiving in Peppertown is a tradition with this family."

It took much ado to get Michael's diverse and lively family to the airport and two thousand miles across the country, but they finally arrived at the white Victorian boarding house where he and Clemmie had first met. Mrs. Grimes, the middle-aged, efficient woman Michael had hired to look after the house met them at the door.

"Daniel and David called to say they would be late. Something about last minute exams at med school." She immediately took charge of Miss Josephine and the three rambunctious Forrest children, ushering them into the kitchen for a snack.

Alone together in the hallway, Michael smiled at Clemmie. "There's another Thanksgiving tradition that has been delayed far too long, my sweet."

They tiptoed upstairs, holding tight to each other's waists. The brass bed shone in the late afternoon sun.

"Remember the first time we made love here, darling?" Clemmie reached for Michael's shirt.

"I'll never forget." In one swift move he divested her of her clothes. "We made Miss Josephine's predictions come true."

Clemmie pulled him onto the bed. "Let's see if it still works."

You'll flip . . . your pages won't!
Read paperbacks *hands-free* with

Book Mate • I

The perfect "mate" for all your romance paperbacks
Traveling • Vacationing • At Work • In Bed • Studying
• Cooking • Eating

Perfect size for all standard paperbacks, this wonderful invention makes reading a pure pleasure! Ingenious design holds paperback books OPEN and FLAT so even wind can't ruffle pages— leaves your hands free to do other things. Reinforced, wipe-clean vinyl-covered holder flexes to let you turn pages without undoing the strap . . . supports paperbacks so well, they have the strength of hardcovers!

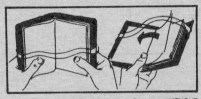

Pages turn WITHOUT opening the strap.

SEE-THROUGH STRAP

Reinforced back stays flat.

Built in bookmark

BOOK MARK

BACK COVER HOLDING STRIP

10" x 7¼", opened.
Snaps closed for easy carrying, too.

Available now. Send your name, address, and zip code, along with a check or money order for just $5.95 + .75¢ for postage & handling (for a total of $6.70) payable to Reader Service to:

Reader Service
Bookmate Offer
901 Fuhrmann Blvd.
P.O. Box 1396
Buffalo, N.Y. 14269-1396

Offer not available in Canada
*New York and Iowa residents add appropriate sales tax.

BM-G

INDULGE A LITTLE–WIN A LOT!

This month's prize:

A VACATION FOR TWO
to Walt Disney World,® Florida!

Are you the Reader Service subscriber who is going to win a *free* vacation to Walt Disney World? The facing page contains two entry forms, as does each of the other books you received in this shipment. Complete and return *all* entry forms—the more you send in, the better your chances of winning!

Then keep your fingers crossed, because you'll find out by October 7, 1989 if you're this month's winner! And if you are, here's what you'll get:

- **Round-trip airfare for two!**
- **7 days/6 nights at a Walt Disney World Resort hotel!**
- **Admissions to The Magic Kingdom® and EPCOT® Center!**
- **A daily cash allowance (as determined by the enclosed "Wallet" scratch-off card)!**

Remember, this is a random drawing *not* open to the general public. The more Official Entry Forms you send in, the better your chances of winning!

Coming next month:
Win a CARIBBEAN CRUISE vacation for 2!
No purchase necessary. See rules for details.

DLIBC-1

MY DARLING CLEMENTINE

When sensible landlord Clementine Brady
wished for a little romance to liven up her quiet
life, she never dreamed that Michael Forrest
would arrive at Brady's Boarding House. His
ardent courtship made her feel as if she were
starring in a fairy tale. But she sensed something
was awry....

Woman-shy Michael had been hurt before, and
he was sure that no female could be as sweet and
as innocent as Clemmie seemed. Vowing to
prove that she wasn't, Michael masqueraded as a
rogue and romanced Clemmie with reckless
abandon. Before long, he discovered he was in
love—and the only one pretending to be
someone he wasn't. True colors revealed, could
he convince Clemmie that he really was her long-
awaited knight in shining armor?

ISBN 0-373-08681-4

0 65373 00225 9

08681

PRINTED IN U.S.A.

W8-BZH-165